2—

Likely Story

Likely Story

David Van Etten

Alfred A. Knopf

New York

Visit us on the Web! www.randomhouse.com/teens

Educators and librarians, for a variety of teaching tools, visit us at www.randomhouse.com/teachers

Library of Congress Cataloging-in-Publication Data
Van Etten, David.
Likely story / David van Etten. — 1st ed.
        p. cm.
Summary: Sixteen-year-old Mallory, daughter of the star of a long-running but faltering soap opera, writes her own soap opera script and becomes deeply involved in the day-to-day life of a Hollywood player, while trying to hold on to some shaky personal relationships.
ISBN 978-0-375-84676-2 (trade) — ISBN 978-0-375-94676-9 (lib. bdg.)
[1. Soap operas—Fiction. 2. Television—Production and direction—Fiction.
3. Interpersonal relations—Fiction. 4. Mothers and daughters—Fiction.
5. Hollywood (Los Angeles, Calif.)—Fiction. I. Title.
PZ7.V2746Li 2008
[Fic]—dc22
2007022724

The text of this book is set in 13-point Galena.

Printed in the United States of America
May 2008
10 9 8 7 6 5 4 3 2 1
First Edition

Random House Children's Books supports the First Amendment and celebrates the right to read.

Likely Story

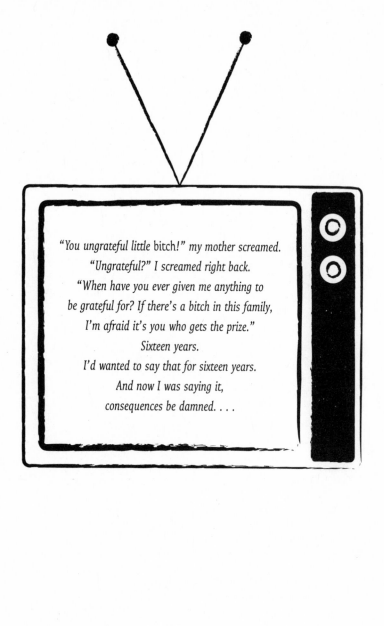

"You ungrateful little bitch!" my mother screamed.
"Ungrateful?" I screamed right back.
"When have you ever given me anything to
be grateful for? If there's a bitch in this family,
I'm afraid it's you who gets the prize."
Sixteen years.
I'd wanted to say that for sixteen years.
And now I was saying it,
consequences be damned. . . .

o n e

My life has been a soap opera since the day I was born.

At the time of my arrival, my mother had been an actress (using that term loosely) on *Good As Gold* for almost ten years. The writers had worked her pregnancy into the story line, and when Mom started going into labor, the director kept the cameras rolling. Mom swears she didn't notice, but if you look at the episode, you can see that she's playing it up, hoping that each contraction will bring her closer to a Daytime Emmy. Luckily, the cameras weren't allowed in the delivery room. But two weeks later, Mom was back at work, on the twelve-by-twelve set that serves as every single hospital room in the fictional town of Shadow Canyon. (If you watch closely, you'll see that only the flowers change.) Immaculately made up, with the whole staff of Shadow Canyon General watching on in admiration, my mother gave birth to me for a second time. And I was there waiting, under the sheet between her legs, for Dr. Lance Singletary to reach in, lift me toward the camera, and utter with complete surprise, "It's a girl, Geneva! It's a girl!"

This was the first time I ever appeared on TV.

It was also the last.

They wanted to keep me. Mom and I were on the cover of *Soap Opera Digest* and *Soap Opera Weekly*. There was a crew from *Entertainment Tonight* taping the *Good As Gold* crew as they taped my second birth. Mom's fan clubs sent thousands of daisies, homemade cards (many of them addressed to Geneva), and home-knit pairs of socks. A network press release dubbed me "the Future Queen of Soapland" and said I was a "star of tomorrow." The hype was stupendous, but clearly I didn't believe my own press. On my second day of taping, I refused to stop crying—big, volcanic wails. The noise was unbearable . . . and, even worse, the way I cried made my face scrunch up. If there's one thing a soap opera will never, ever tolerate, it's a scrunched-up, uncute face, even on a sixteen-day-old baby.

A supermodel pair of baby twins was brought in, and I was sent home with a nanny. Four months later, *Good As Gold* viewers would watch as Geneva's infant daughter, Diamond, was abducted by Geneva's escaped-convict ex-lover, a former priest named Rance who had sixteen personalities (ten of whom were battling sex addiction). When Diamond was found six months later by the lone member of Shadow Canyon's police force, she had miraculously transformed into a breast-budding twelve-year-old starlet—a fact that none of the citizens of Shadow Canyon (not even the clairvoyant ones) ever noticed.

In the past sixteen years, Diamond has been abducted six times, has died once, has fallen in love twice with people who were later revealed to be her relatives, has had three bouts of amnesia, has been in a coma twice, has eloped once, has broken off two engagements, has had her debutante debut ruined once by an earthquake and once by a dead best friend, has twice fallen into the hands of a coven of witches, has been locked in the trunk of a car six times, has pulled a gun on someone fourteen times, has had a gun pulled on her twenty-two times, and has had near-death experiences eight times (twice from drowning, twice in a car crash, once in a plane crash, once after being stabbed by her lover-slash-long-lost-stepbrother, once in childbirth, and once—I swear to god—from slipping on a patch of black ice, which was later revealed to have been put there by her diabolically scheming half sister/stepmother).

The one thing Diamond and I have in common: Neither of us knows who our father is. Everyone has a theory. Personally, I'd like a name.

Really, it's only compared to Diamond's life that my own life seems ordinary. By most other standards, it's still pretty messed up.

In the past sixteen years, my mother has been engaged four times, has been married three times, and has been sued for palimony twice. We have lived in eleven different places—one for each engagement and marriage, one carriage house, one apartment, one extended stay at the Beverly Wilshire hotel, and one extended stay at an "exhaustion clinic" (chosen because it had day care). I have attended six different schools, have faced off against either nineteen or twenty nannies—I've lost count—and have met at least five different men who may or may not be my father.

It's been a lot to deal with, mostly on my own. Only two

things have remained constant. The first is the way I'm treated at school. It doesn't matter which school, whether it's full of stoners or preps or aspiring actresses or nuns. They're pretty much the same once my mom's identity is revealed. I've put up with it all. "Hey, your mom is sleeping with the mayor of Shadow Canyon even though he's married to her sister!" "Hey, how'd your mom like having sex with a guy who ended up being a ghost?" "Hey, isn't your mom the one who was abducted by aliens and came back with a pack of dynamite strapped to her bra on a brainwashed mission to blow up the Shadow Canyon Mother-Daughter Fashion Show?"

Yes, that's my mom.

Uh-huh.

You got me.

Please stop.

You'd think it would be enough to make me loathe soap operas. But, really, I can't hate them too much, since the second big constant in my life has been the *Good As Gold* set. The only babysitter or nanny I ever tolerated was Gina, my mother's makeup person (which makes her a pretty big constant, as well). Not because she let me play dress-up or taught me how to use mascara (I still don't). No, I loved Gina because she would let me sit in the space beneath my mother's makeup table so I could read as much as I wanted. I would alternate between *Little Women* and all the gossip magazines; a lot of the time I learned more about my mother from *Us Weekly* than I did from our us-weekly dinners. I also loved to read my mother's scripts, because each one was more melodramatic than the next. At school I learned addition, subtraction, multiplication, and long division. After school I learned seduction, distraction, manipulation, and long indecision. You'd think it would have made me a little slut. But ultimately it just made me want to write about little sluts.

The older I got, the more I realized how ridiculous *Good As Gold* was. Time moved very, very slowly in the scripts—usually a whole week's worth of episodes would take place in about three hours of Shadow Canyon time. And in that three hours there'd be everything from murder, sex, and betrayal to feral-cat attacks and gratuitously half-naked coed swim meets. The characters I loathed the most were the teenagers, because they never found the time to go to school or do anything outside their little world. If anything, they were just extensions of their parents' plotlines. Even when it got a little interesting—ooh, Diamond's dabbling in lesbianism; wow, Carter's become addicted to *champagne*—the plots seemed to exist so the town elders could have more Daytime Emmy Moments of shock! outrage! and grief! As soon as the parents stopped wringing their hands over the trouble the teens had gotten into, the teens were off in search of another form of trouble. (For whatever reason, the *Good As Gold* writers loved to threaten the teen characters with electrocution. Nothing like a run-in with an open wire to boost ratings.)

It was comedy, but nobody seemed in on the joke.

At first I kept my mouth shut. Then I couldn't take it anymore.

The big breakthrough came on a day that nobody was expecting even a small breakthrough. It was midnight after a long day of eleventh grade (for me) and a long day of shooting

7

(for Mom), and Mom was watching herself on TiVo. She'll never admit she does this, but what can I say—she's addicted to herself.

The scene was pretty harmless, as *Good As Gold* scenes go. Geneva was talking to yet another ex, Colt, who'd been blinded in a car accident that was caused by either an on-coming truck (driven by Geneva?) or a UFO (driven by Geneva?).

                    GENEVA
              We can't do this.

                     COLT
          Geneva, you're the only woman
            I would want to see . . .
               if I <u>could</u> see.

                    GENEVA
            You may be the blind one,
          Colt, but I'm the one who's
          truly been blind. Blind to
              the consequences.

                     COLT
                Hold me.

                    GENEVA
          I can't! Not with Vance in
             the other room!

COLT
If you won't hold me, then
I'll hold you.

That's really all it took to get Geneva into bed. Although at this point in Mom's career—much to her distress—Geneva always seemed to fall into bed with her clothes fully on.

"Did you really just say, 'You may be the blind one, but I'm the one who's truly been blind'?" I asked.

From the resulting silence, I figured Mom hadn't heard me—she was too busy studying the way she looked as Colt unbridled her. But after the scene was over (which was about ten seconds later, since soap-opera scenes never last longer than it takes to unbutton a shirt), Mom paused the TiVo.

"What?" she said, annoyed.

I knew I was breaking her routine. When Mom watched the TiVo, she always took precise mental notes. Not about what she could do to improve her performance—no, more like who she could blame for whatever was wrong. Her co-stars, the writers, the lighting director, the guy from catering who wouldn't stop putting potato chips on the snack table—if Mom wasn't hitting her mark, someone had to burn. I myself never felt too far out of the range of her blame. My whole existence threw her off.

"Don't you ever get sick of the crap lines?" I said to her now. "Don't you ever want to sound like a real person instead of someone on a soap opera?"

"A *real person*? Are you the expert on *real people* now?" Mom challenged, using her best vodka voice. Absolut bitch.

I continued. "It's like you're in this world full of Hallmark sayings, although Hallmark would never, ever use any of them on a card. *Dear Colt. I'm so sorry that you're blind. But I'm the one who's truly been blind. Come see me sometime for a cure. Love, Geneva.*"

"It works" was all Mom had to say to that.

"If it works so well, why are your ratings down?"

The minute I said it, I knew I'd crossed the line . . . right into my mother's militarized zone. I was allowed to trash the dialogue—she'd only blame the writers for the purple prose, even though she was the one who stuck the quill so far deep into the purple ink, especially when she "improvised." I could even, if she was in a good mood, make fun of a costume or the name of a character. But I was never allowed to discuss anything to do with aging, appearance, the Daytime Emmy she'd never won, or bad ratings.

If it had been an episode of *Good As Gold,* she would have slapped me. But instead she unpaused her TiVo and turned back to her show. She even turned up the volume a little, to punctuate the point.

I figured if she could act like an adolescent, then I (the actual adolescent) could, too. So I went to my room, slammed the door, and pulled out my journal to fire off a few lines. But even that didn't satisfy me.

I had a blog that I used every now and then—it was pretty low-key, and I thought maybe a dozen people had read it. It seemed like a safe space. So before I could think too much about it, I started to vent.

Why are soap operas so fake? Who the hell wants to spend an hour every day watching amnesiac nymphomaniacs who speak like aliens from the planet Melodrama? What about real problems? What about real drama? Real life is contrived enough as it is. Wouldn't it be great to have a soap opera about people you actually cared about? Wouldn't it be revolutionary to revolve a show around all the messed-up crap that actually happens to us instead of all this make-believe crap? My friends' stories—anybody's stories—are about a hundred times more compelling than anything you can find on the TV at three o'clock. You want to know why soap operas are going the way of the dinosaur? It's because we relate to the characters about as much as we would relate to a dinosaur. If I had my own show, I'd be able to prove to you how right I am.

I figured nobody would read it.

It ended up that two people did.

My best friend, Amelia, called me about two minutes after I posted it.

"So you and your mom got into a fight again." (That was her version of hello.)

"I mentioned her ratings."

"Whoa! Did you happen to mention that she needs a new face-lift, too?"

"I couldn't. The TV was too loud. I think the last face-lift might have accidentally covered up her ears."

"It's not fair, you know. I wish I could make fun of my parents' ratings, too. All parents should have ratings to make fun of."

Amelia and I were somewhere between being old friends and new friends, meaning we'd known each other for about a year, ever since I'd moved to Cloverdale, my latest school. (My mother tended to send me to a new school every time we moved house, like getting a new pair of shoes to match a new dress.) I didn't know what she was complaining about—her parents were pretty cool in a carpool-and-curfew kind of way. But they were never enough for Amelia, who wanted them to be a part of the Hollywood side of LA. She had dreams of being a big star, and her parents (both of them English teachers) didn't want her to hit the firmament until she finished high school and college.

"Well," she said to me now, "if I had a few million dollars, I'd definitely give you a show to run. And I'd watch it every single day, if I wasn't out on auditions."

"Oh, don't worry," I told her. "If I have a show of my own, you'll get to be the lead. There's no way I could do it without you."

She cheered around that, and we moved on to other topics—boys, classes, blah blah blah. The whole show idea would've probably ended there.

But then I got the next call.

It was Donald, my mother's agent. He'd been my mother's agent for as long as anyone could remember and was, as far as I could tell, the only straight guy who'd survived knowing my mother for that long without being eaten by her praying-mantis side.

"Hello, Mallory," he said. Unlike most people in LA, he always said hello.

"Hi, Donald. What's up?"

"I saw your blog." He said the word *blog* as if it was something out of a science-fiction movie. "I love your idea. Do you have a bible?"

Now, if I hadn't grown up on a soap-opera set, this question probably would have thrown me—was Donald going to ask me to repent for my sins? Go check the Testaments to find some inspiration there?

But he wasn't talking about *the* Bible. He was talking about *a* bible. Every show had one—the list of characters and plots and relationships and settings that acted as the foundation for all the stories the writers came up with. The longer a show ran, the longer and more complicated its bible became. At the beginning, it was usually about fifty pages and had enough characters and story ideas for a year's worth of episodes.

Right then, of course, my "bible" consisted of exactly one ranting blog entry. But I wasn't about to tell Donald that.

"Yeah, I have a bible," I said.

He paused to think. Ever since I was a little kid, I'd imagined that if thoughts could have sounds, Donald's thoughts would be like ice cubes clinking in a glass. There was something cold about the way he processed things, but also something a little musical.

Finally, he said, "Can you send it to me tomorrow? It's a long shot, but I think the network's been looking for something like this. And I'm having lunch with Stu Eisenhorn."

Stu Eisenhorn was the president of the network on which *Good As Gold* aired. As far as I could tell, he'd never been jilted by, entangled with, or enraptured by my mother. Which was a big plus.

"I can get it to you first thing," I said.

"That's my girl!" Donald replied. Then he wished me good night.

As if I was going to get any sleep. I figured I had about six hours to come up with an entire soap opera.

The first thing I needed was a town name. The first word that came to mind was *Deception,* for obvious reasons.

That sounded like a start.

Deception . . .

I needed another noun.

Deception Mountain.

It sounded like a place where gay spies retired. Or a twisted Disneyland ride.

Deception Valley.

Like a bad salad dressing.

Deception Hills.

Fake boobs.

Deception Ranch.

Another bad salad dressing.

I looked at my bulletin board and saw photos of me

and Amelia; photos of me and my sort-of-maybe-part-time boyfriend, Keith; tickets from old concerts; a backstage pass to my old friend Aaron's concert at the Hollywood Bowl.

Backstage pass. Pass.

Deception Pass.

Bingo.

Now all I needed were about a dozen characters, two dozen plotlines, and a map of the town.

This time I looked up at my shelves. Specifically, I looked at the row of eleven notebooks on the very top shelf, my entire journaled life since the age of twelve.

Surely, there was enough reality there to be turned into a soap opera.

I put my laptop atop my lap and started flipping through all the years of passionate handwriting. It only took a few memory flashes to get me started.

This wasn't going to be *based on a true story,* with the *true story* being my life. Yeah, I started with autobiography, but I quickly diverged from that. I wanted this to be about real people with real problems. (Life with my mother did *not* count as real.) I started with the basic shape of all storytelling—the romantic triangle. This was something I knew about. So I plotted: Ryan is in love with Sarah, who is best friends with Jacqueline, who is in love with Ryan. Sarah does the honorable, self-defeating thing and lets Ryan go with Jacqueline, even though Sarah secretly wishes it was her. The complications start to add up. The whole town gets involved.

Unlike soaps where one catastrophe follows another and every character is a different shade of psycho, this would be about normal people and all of the messes they get into. It would be a likely story. That would be the big thing about it. And it could even be the title, just so people knew where we stood. *Likely Story.*

I typed through the night.

And that's how my second life in soap operas began.

"I am so in love with you," Keith said.
"If only you didn't have a girlfriend," I replied,
trying not to let the sadness in my voice
edge out the happiness of the moment.
"Yeah," he said, running his hand over my arm.
"If only."

t w o

"You did *what*?" Amelia said after I told her the whole story.

"I e-mailed it to Donald before I came to school. We'll see."

We were heading into Mrs. Finch's Universal Themes class. That was the thing about Cloverdale—it didn't believe in simple classes like "English" or "Math." No, my schedule was full of Universal Themes, Logic and Equations, Heroic Tales, and other Incredibly Vague Nouns With Occasional Adjectives. The students, for the most part, liked to show up to class stoned, so I'm sure it all seemed very deep to them. To me, it was like drowning in mental mayonnaise.

"I'd love to talk about *gestalt* today," Mrs. Finch announced after the class bell rang. "Who'd like to start talking about *gestalt*?"

Amanda Hooper saved the day, as she always did, by knowing exactly what Mrs. Finch was talking about. She went on about Freud and Nietzsche and the "gestalt paradigm." Some of the stoners nodded, but the rest of us couldn't have been more lost if we were on a desert island.

"What about you, Mallory?" Mrs. Finch asked. "Where do you locate *gestalt* in these texts?"

Over the years, I'd seen my mother do hundreds of interviews, and after a while, I realized that she'd discovered the secret to the successful answering of questions: No matter what question is being asked, you can use it to answer a completely different question. For example, if she was asked, "Has motherhood been hard for you to balance?" she could answer, "Not as hard as taping my shocking love scene with Dashell Blakemore, which will air next Thursday—*everyone* should watch!" (This is, I've since learned, called "media training"— you think it means that you're trained to work with the media, but, really, you're the one training the media to be a slave to your whims.)

I decided to use my secondhand media training now with Mrs. Finch.

"I think *Invisible Man* shows us that you don't have to be invisible to be invisible," I said. "It's enough just to be poor."

"A good point!" Mrs. Finch cheered. "And what else?"

"It would seem, Mrs. Finch, that invisibility is a Universal Theme. I'm sure it can even be found in Harry Potter."

"The invisibility cloak!" one of our stoner kings, Leaf (not his real name), called out.

"I see," Mrs. Finch said. And she was about to say something else, too—but then my cell phone rang and interrupted everything.

I didn't usually have my cell phone on in class—Mrs. Finch was a big confiscation fan, and my phone meant too much to me to risk losing it. But I was anxious about Donald's lunch with Stu Eisenhorn, and I was afraid if I set the phone to silent I would miss something important.

I looked at the screen. It was Donald's number.

"I have to get this," I said.

Next to me, Amelia let out a string of excited little shrieks. Everyone was looking at me—especially Mrs. Finch.

"I'll take it outside," I said. As if to explain, I added, "It's an agent."

Mrs. Finch called after me, but I didn't care—Departure for Good Reason was, I imagined, a Universal Theme as well. I'd find a passage from *Invisible Man* or Harry Potter or whatever to back it up.

"Donald," I said, "talk to me."

"Hello, Mallory. I hope I'm not interrupting anything."

I looked at the door to Mrs. Finch's classroom. "Nope. Nothing." I found it sweet that Donald could never remember that I was still in school. Most of the children he dealt with had on-set tutors.

"Good! I have news for you."

"Good news?"

"Great news!"

At this point I was nearly shrieking, too. And I am *not* a shrieker.

"Whatwhatwhat?"

"I pitched," Donald told me. "He swung. It connected."

"In non-baseball terms?"

"Stu Eisenhorn really loves *Likely Story*. If there'd been a green light in the restaurant, I believe he would've green-lit it on the spot. He thinks it's a great story, and, just as important, he thinks *you're* a great story. 'She's the next generation of soaps,' he kept saying. It was my phrase, but I'm letting him think he came up with it himself."

"So what does this mean?" I asked.

"It means we're talking with the daytime president tomorrow. I've started spreading the word, and the buzz is already cresting. Greta from Page Seven has already called me. Twice. And that old battle-ax hasn't covered your mother since her recipe for the *Page Seven Celebrity Soap-Opera Cookbook* was such a disaster."

"You couldn't have seriously expected Mom to know the difference between a teaspoon and a tablespoon. . . ."

"I think it was more the fact that she didn't know eggs could be separated."

"She thought some eggs had whites and others had yolks. Is that really so hard to believe?"

"I had to work very, very hard to prevent Greta from putting that into her column. But now she's all over you. *And you don't even have a show yet.*"

"But I will?" I asked.

"Yes, you will." Donald sounded sure of it, and that was good enough for me. Donald had been the one to tell Mom to take the part in *Good As Gold* instead of a two-minute role in an Indiana Jones rip-off movie. Mom had said he was crazy, that she was made for the big screen. But his instincts trumped hers, and, as a result, I was a soap-opera baby instead of the daughter of a straight-to-video starlet.

"What time's the meeting?" I asked him.

"Ten. Can you do that?"

"Of course I can." School? What's school?

"Whatever you do, *don't* dress up. Look your age. That's what we're selling."

I figured I could handle that.

We talked a little longer, but I knew I had to get back into the classroom soon. Not because of Mrs. Finch—I couldn't care less about Mrs. Finch. But I was sure that Amelia was going to explode if I didn't give her the update right away.

All eyes were on me when I walked back in. All I had to do was smile and Amelia was out of her chair, hugging me, jumping us both up and down. That somehow made it more real. This was really happening. I was in shock, but, luckily, Amelia expressed enough excitement for both of us.

"Your show! They're going to give you a show!" she cried.

"Our show," I told her. "*Our* show." And I meant it. I knew right away that it would be much more fun if we did it together—the writer and the star. I had no desire whatsoever to be in front of the camera. Amelia could do that. We would support each other, be there for each other, experience it all together.

Mrs. Finch tried to regain control of the class, but it was too far gone now. I didn't want to tell everyone the exact idea for *Likely Story* yet—I didn't want to jinx it. So instead we talked about favorite soap-opera "themes," and everyone had a thing or two to say. Leaf, it appeared, was partial to twins separated at birth. Amanda liked it when nightmares foretold plot twists. Amelia was a sucker for people returning from the dead—I made a mental note of that. Even Mrs. Finch made a contribution, saying that more than resurrection, she liked it when characters were reincarnated from dead relatives or ancient monarchs. I made a mental note of that, too, but toward the back of my mental notepad.

I tried to play it cool for the rest of the school day. Now that Amelia (and our whole Universal Themes class) knew, there were two other people I was dying to tell—Keith and Gina.

Keith was waiting for me by his car, an old Ford Mustang he'd lovingly restored by hand. As usual, my body temperature rose a few degrees when I saw him, and my pulse got that fluster-flutter that comes from liking someone you're not entirely sure you should like. With some guys, you feel like it's destined to be. With others, life makes you work for it.

"Hey, sailor," he called out to me. We had this thing—we always called each other nicknames, but we could never use the same nickname twice. It was like we were auditioning them and having fun until we found the ones that stuck.

"Hey, bugle boy," I replied. He held his arms open a little, and I walked right into them.

"Mmmmm," he said, pulling me a little closer before kissing me. I loved the way he *mmmmm*ed. Like every time he saw me I was slipping off a negligee.

"Guess what," I said.

"What?"

"Apparently, you're kissing the future of soap operas."

He kissed me again. "I knew there was a different taste to it today. Yes, a little soaplike. And opera! I definitely taste opera."

"I'm serious," I said, although I didn't feel the need to be. Keith tended to unserious me.

I told him what had happened so far. He didn't seem to understand most of it, but that was more than okay with me; there were enough people in my life who kneeled before Nielsen ratings. It was nice to have a guy who couldn't name or recognize the *Desperate Housewives* cast members. Not even Teri Hatcher.

"I'm so proud of you," he whispered.

Was this the first time in my life that anyone had said such a thing to me?

Possibly.

Probably.

But that wasn't all.

"I am so in love with you," Keith said.

"If only you didn't have a girlfriend," I replied, trying not to let the sadness in my voice edge out the happiness of the moment.

"Yeah," he said, running his hand over my arm. "If only."

I couldn't believe I'd brought up Erika at a moment like this. Couldn't I leave her out of it, just for a nanosecond of us-ness?

No. Clearly I couldn't. She was always there.

I felt bad for saying it. So I did the natural thing: I made it even worse.

"You don't have to be with her, you know?" I said. "It could just be us."

Proud of me now, Keith?

No, I didn't think so.

"Mallory," he said, stepping away from me, getting out his keys. "You know it's complicated."

Complicated because Erika was going through "hard

25

times." Complicated because she didn't go to our school, which made it easier for him to be with me when he wanted to be. Complicated because I was the one making him choose, since she had no idea I existed. Complicated because she came first.

Complicated because I was willing to kiss him anyway.

I knew he wasn't leaving me (not at that moment) for her. I knew he had to get to work, waiting tables at California Pizza Kitchen in order to afford gas for his Mustang. I knew I had to let him go serve the pizza-needing masses.

But still I wanted to say "stay."

I always wanted to say "stay."

"I'll call you tonight for a pep talk," he said.

"For what?" I asked.

"For the meeting tomorrow. Duh, kitten!"

We kissed once more, but it was a rushed kiss.

I didn't watch him drive away, but I had to make an effort not to.

I tried to get back into the groove of my good news. I couldn't wait to tell Gina.

I drove to the lot where *Good As Gold* was taped, and Max, the guard, waved me right in with a thumbs-up sign. The lot was a leftover from the studio heyday of the 1940s, when even the places on the lot that never showed up on film were designed to feel larger than life. It was only when you got deep backstage, to the offices and dressing rooms, that things seemed a little less grand and a lot more human.

Gina was where I usually could find her—in my mother's dressing room, prepping for Mom's next scene. True to form, she was ironing a kimono when I walked in. Since a kimono would be way too "ethnic" for an out-of-house scene, I figured my mother was going to be taping in one of the three bedroom sets sometime soon. The clothes were really the wardrobe person's responsibility, but Gina was the only person on the set that my mother trusted.

I was about to blurt out my news to Gina, but she beat me to it.

"Mallory! I always knew you could do it!" she cried, putting the iron down to give me a big hug. I figured that whether or not the show went through, getting this much affection was definitely worth it.

"It's not a done deal yet," I cautioned.

Gina shook her head. "Don't think that way, sweetie. It's a *fantastic* idea, and the tidal wave's on your side. The network needs this more than you could know. And who better to do it?"

Her beaming was like chocolate to me.

"There's just one thing . . . ," she went on. But before she could tell me what that one thing was, it barged right through the door.

"*How dare you!*" it yelled.

"Hi, Mom," I said.

Gina didn't know what to do. Then my mother released a guttural "*OUT!*" and there wasn't really a question of which direction Gina would soon be heading. She looked to me, and I'm sure she would have stayed and faced my mother's wrath if I'd needed her to. But I told her it was okay, and she left me alone with Soapzilla.

"I guess you've heard the news," I said, trying to stay calm.

"The *news*? Is that what it is? You go around my back to my agent—"

"He was the one who called me—"

"*You go around my back to my agent and manipulate your way onto my network*—"

"Now wait a second. It's hardly your—"

"*And you don't even tell me.* I have the president of the network call me to tell me about my daughter's idea, and I just have to *play along* and pretend that I have *some idea of what he's talking about.* I sit there and have him tell me that you are going to be the one to rescue daytime drama *from the brink. Of. Extinction.*"

"This isn't about you, Mom," I told her. Forgetting, of course, that there was no way she could define a single situation without being at the center of it.

"Not about me?!? You can't be serious! This is *entirely* about me."

That was it. I'd had it.

"Stop it," I told her. "Just stop it!"

"You ungrateful little *bitch*!" my mother screamed.

"Ungrateful?" I screamed right back. "When have you ever given me anything to be grateful for? If there's a bitch in this family, I'm afraid it's you who gets the prize."

Sixteen years.

I'd wanted to say that for sixteen years.

And now I was saying it, consequences be damned. . . .

"Rest assured, I am *not* going to let this happen," she said.

"I don't think it's up to you," I replied.

"I am your mother!"

"Unfortunate, isn't it?"

Once again, she looked like she was ready to give me a soap-opera slap—it wouldn't have actually hit me, but it would have looked very dramatic. Either that or she was going to rip all my hair out, one chunk at a time.

I was saved by the bell.

The ring of her cell phone, to be exact.

She looked at the number, then quickly picked up.

Suddenly it was like she was a different person. A normal, calm, kind, funny person.

"Greta!" she chirped. "How wonderful to hear from you! . . . Yes, it's been far too long! . . . I absolutely couldn't be more thrilled about it, dear. Mallory's always been my shining light. . . . Inspiration? Oh, Greta, I just hope like every mother that I've been able to teach her all the things she'll need to be a huge success!"

She was looking at her makeup table when she said all this. Then she looked up into the mirror and saw me perched in the background. With a swipe of her hand, she told me to get lost. This didn't even count as a truce—just a pause.

I said good-bye to Gina, who had been waiting outside the door. The great thing about her was that she never apologized for my mother; she knew it was my mother's job to do that. Instead, she gave me a look and another hug that made me know she understood what I was going through . . . and she also understood I would be getting through it fine. I was lucky: Even if my own mother was a horror show, at least I had Gina waiting in the wings. When I was little, I would dream that she'd adopt me. Sometimes I would even sneak into the backseat of her car and hide there as she drove back to her home and her family. She never seemed too surprised when I popped up at the end of the ride; she'd call my mother, invite me to dinner, then drive me back home at the end of the night. I always begged to sleep over, preferably for good.

I knew if I'd asked her to take me with her for a home-cooked meal, she wouldn't have argued. But I didn't want to impose, didn't want to bring my own agitation into her house. So I headed back to my own home. For the rest of the after-noon and into the night, I stayed in my room, studying what I'd written the night before. If this was going to happen, I had to be an expert on my own material. Even Amelia's and Keith's and Donald's pep-talk phone calls didn't make me less ner-vous; if anything, they increased the pressure, since I wanted to keep Amelia and Keith and Donald happy along with me.

If there was one thing I was sure of, it was that tomorrow morning's meeting would be important.

If there was one thing I wasn't sure of, it was that tomor-row morning's meeting would go well.

Not only was the network's daytime president a notorious hard-ass.

He was also my mother's third ex-husband.

"Sometimes you have to betray the people
who are close to you," Richard told me.
Then he added, as an afterthought,
"For their own good."
I didn't know what to do.

three

"Mallory!" Trip Carver exclaimed, standing up behind his desk to shake my hand. "It's so wonderful to see you!"

And all I could think was: *Liar!*

Trip Carver was the kind of guy who only smiled when he was tearing someone apart. I guess my mother was attracted to that . . . for a time. She and Trip had dated for only about seven months before getting hitched—"a marriage made in daytime heaven," according to *Soap Opera Digest.* Well, as far as I could tell, the only thing the marriage had in common with heaven was that a lot of things died to get there. In public, Mom and Trip were tuxedo-and-gown compatible. But in private, they were scissors and rock. They "fixed" this by eliminating private contact altogether. Trip worked late, Mom worked early, and any overlap was barely bearable. I was thirteen and had already seen two husbands come and go—I had no desire to attach to Trip and he had no desire to attach to me. If we saw each other, I'd say hello and he'd nod; that's how it was.

Then Trip cheated on Mom. Not with his secretary or his best friend's wife, but with his best friend's wife's secretary, who spelled her name *S-I-N-D-Y*. When Mom found out, she threw things. In between ducking and picking up pieces of shattered statuary, Trip looked bored. The divorce papers soon appeared, and Mom and I were moving to a new house again. Mom blabbed about Trip's tryst to the fan sites, and Trip's lawyers had to work extra hard to convince him not to fire her on the spot. Breaking up with the boss had actually given her *more* job security—only someone like Mom could pull that off. Now when they saw each other, Trip was always coldly polite and Mom always asked him how Sindy was, even though Sindy had flown the well-decorated coop months ago.

Trip looked a little grayer than he'd been when we'd shared a house. But other than that, he was the same, acting like his soul wore a suit.

"I love *Likely Story*," he told us, his eyes alternating between Donald and me. "Absolutely love it. One of the freshest pitches we've seen in years."

The daytime VP, a spare woman named Celene Thimble, nodded behind him. I made my face devoid of all hope and/or excitement. I knew if I seemed too eager, Trip would take advantage of it.

"So what're you thinking?" Donald asked.

"Well, as you know, we're announcing a new lineup soon, and I'd like this to be a part of it. We're willing to budget the first steps and then go from there. Casting will be crucial, of course. And we need a good show runner."

He reached out his hand, and an assistant sprang from the side of the room with a folder in his hand. Like me, the assistant was keeping all expression off his face. He was wearing an expensive suit, but he looked like he was playing dress-up. He couldn't have been more than five years older than me.

Trip took a photo out of the folder and put it on the desk for the rest of us to see.

It was a total glamour head shot—every hair in place, head tilted slightly to let the light add some attractive shadows. The guy in it was sexy, no doubt about it—his eyes gleamed with bold intensity. *Confidence*—that's what he had. The kind you wanted to make out with.

There was one problem, though. He was easily in his late twenties, maybe even thirty. There was no way anybody would buy him as Ryan, the male lead on my show.

"Isn't he a little old for Ryan?" I asked.

Trip chuckled condescendingly.

"That's not an actor," he said. "That's going to be your executive producer, Richard Showalter. We've had our eye on him for months now. He's a little bit HBO, a little bit MTV. Like you, he knows what kids like. I think between the two of you, we'll get a truly groundbreaking show."

This was daytime TV—I knew Trip didn't really want "groundbreaking." He wanted "commercial"—but since I was "creative" (which, to the soul-suits, also meant "touchy," "unreasonable," and "freaky"), he thought I needed to hear "groundbreaking."

"As long as people watch it," I said. "That's what I want."

Trip seemed pleased by this.

"We'll set up a meeting with you and Richard," he said. Then he pulled another photo out of his folder.

This one wasn't a head shot. It was this completely creative black-and-white photograph of the most beautiful guy in the history of creation. He was walking through Central Park, unaware that his photo was being taken.

"Sweet Jesus," I said. I couldn't help myself.

Trip nodded. "He looks even better in color," he told me.

"He's Ryan," I said. "Exactly."

"*Exactly*," Trip echoed.

"But who is he? Really, I mean?"

"His name is Dallas Grant, and he's a senior at Juilliard in New York. We've literally seen him stop traffic—some poor girl was driving down Broadway and got into a fender bender because she couldn't help watching him cross the street. One of our execs saw this, then called a photographer to get some shots. Our Juilliard scouts say he's a very promising actor . . . and he's about a hundred thou in debt for school. We can't believe that nobody else has gotten to him yet. But we're already on it."

I couldn't stop thinking how perfect this boy was for Ryan, my brooding, darkly mysterious hero-slash-antihero. It would make perfect sense for all of Deception Pass's female residents to fall desperately in love with him, especially Sarah and Jacqueline, the other points in the romantic triangle.

But I also couldn't help thinking: *He's so beautiful that I'm already intimidated by him.* His beauty wasn't the simple blank-slateness of a male model in an underwear ad. No. It had complexity. Beguiling complexity.

The room was silent, and it took me a second to realize that Trip must have asked me a question while I was staring at Dallas's photo.

"So you approve?" Donald prompted.

"Absolutely," I said.

Trip then showed a few actresses for the female leads, Jacqueline and Sarah. I narrowed down a few candidates for Jacqueline. As for Sarah . . . well, that was Amelia's part. Since I wasn't about to tell them that yet, I said, "I have someone else in mind for Sarah," and left it at that. Trip nodded and said we would make casting decisions at a later date.

He still hadn't said what my position was going to be, exactly. I wasn't shocked that he wanted to bring in an executive producer—as much as the show was going to be my creation, I didn't know the first thing about budgets, finance, production costs, and anything else involving dollar signs and stress. If I was going to raise this baby, I needed someone else to figure out how to pay for it.

At the very least, I wanted head-writer and creator credit. Trip was no fool—he knew my soap-opera lineage was as much of a hook as anything I'd written.

I figured I'd let Donald iron everything out. All I needed was Trip to get us going.

Trip started to speak in his second language—it's called Demographics—and I only half listened as he talked about how advertisers were trying to capture the 18 to 35 range now more than ever, and how the network's strength had always been 55 plus, especially in Daytime. (When Trip said "Daytime," it was always with a capital *D*.) The prime-time programming was already trying to skew younger; *Likely Story* would be a "natural extension" of that.

As long as I could cast Dallas Grant and Amelia, I was happy.

Finally, the meeting was over. The assistant made the motion to lead us all away, but Trip asked if I could stay back for a second. Everybody else filed out.

"You realize," Trip said to me, his blue-charcoal eyes unwavering, "that we're going to have to sell the hell out of you to make this work. You've always been your mother's daughter, but now you're *really* going to be your mother's daughter. I don't want you suddenly thinking you're going to be able to distance yourself from that."

This didn't bother me in the least. "I've put up with my mother all these years," I told Trip. "I might as well get something out of that."

This time his smile was a kind I hadn't seen him use before—a smile of respect.

"Good," he said. "I'll tell you this—you are getting in on your merits, since your bible is better than ninety-nine percent of the dreck that makes its way into this office. But it's your name that's going to make this an easy sell."

Now it was my turn to smile.

"That's fine," I said.

Sensing our meeting was now over, I stood up to leave. Trip stood, too, and saved his last words until I was almost out the door.

"Mallory," he said, and I turned back around to face him. "You know that I hate your mother."

I didn't say anything.

"And you know," he continued, "that your mother is going to hate this."

I nodded, showing him I understood completely.

Two wrongs might not make a right . . . but two hates could definitely get a soap opera into production.

I was set.

I trusted Donald to work out all the details. A few days later, there was a big headline in *Daily Variety*:

SOAP OPERA PRINCESS GETS HER KINGDOM

I didn't particularly like being called a princess. But I *loved* the idea of having a kingdom.

The article said that *Likely Story* was on a fast track.

It also said that Richard Showalter was in negotiations to be executive producer.

I figured I had to meet him soon.

First, though, Amelia and I had to celebrate.

Other girls probably would have thrown a party. Word would have spread through school, and soon dozens—if not hundreds—of people would have been crowded into my house, spilling drinks on the carpet and making out in the available enclosed spaces (and probably some of the open ones).

I didn't like to celebrate that way.

I had a sense that Amelia might have been into a party, but she was nice enough to indulge my antisocial behavior. After the news was released into the world, a few kids at school kissed up to try to get roles or, at the very least, passes onto the set. But most acted like I'd proven undeniably what they'd always thought to be true: I was a mutant from the planet Soap Opera and had spawned from my mother to spread salacious contrivance throughout the televised universe. To give an example: One football player in my Logic and Equations class yelled out, "Hey, Mallory, is there going to be a lot of hot evil-twin action on your show?" and the other people in the room laughed. At me, not with me.

I figured I would have my revenge soon enough. In my soap-opera world, all of the football players were going to be impotent.

In fairness, there were a few kids—mostly soapfan girls and gayboys—who were happy for me. But Amelia was the only one who traveled over the moon with me. So I figured our celebration should be a private one. On a whim, I booked us a room at the W—not a suite, just a room—so we could hang out and watch bad cable and eat ice cream without worrying that anyone (particularly any soap stars of a certain age) would interrupt. One of the only perks of being with Mom when she was on publicity tours was getting to spend the days in fancy hotel rooms; I loved having temporary possession of the bed, of the fancy shampoos, of the bathrobes. Staying in a hotel room was like being in a place where you held only the bare minimum of responsibility. I could relax there in a way that I could never relax at home. Plus, the W had special meaning to me. It was the same hotel that Trip had gone to when he'd cheated on Mom, so I figured it was a fitting place to celebrate. I planned to be within eyeshot when Mom saw it listed on her credit card.

After I arrived at the front desk, the desk manager told me my guest had already arrived and gone up. She winked at me then, and I wondered if she thought Amelia and I were a couple.

I myself started to wonder when I opened the door to the

room and found it lit entirely in candlelight. Before I could think *fire hazard,* Keith appeared in front of the bed, dressed only in a white T and his boxers.

"Surprise!" he said. And I'll admit it—I was surprised.

In between kisses, he explained that Amelia had granted him an hour in the room with me, and he planned to make the most of it.

For us, "the most of it" didn't mean *all of it*—the rose petals on the bed were the only things that were going to be deflowered tonight. There were lots of reasons for this, but the primary one was named Erika.

We rolled around on the bed for a while and made out, kissing and grasping and keeping all our clothes on. A lot of the time, I was really into it—I could lose myself from any other thoughts besides the heat of him and the heat of me and the heat of us as we kissed and rolled and felt. But every now and then, flashes of Erika would intrude. I would think of him kissing her. Sleeping with her. Doing everything he was doing with me, only with her. Liking it more. Going further. Not thinking of me.

I didn't stop, but part of me stopped. And then it wasn't just Erika I was seeing. No, lying there in the hotel bed, Keith kissing my neck, pulling my shirt aside to kiss his way to my shoulder . . . suddenly it was Dallas Grant's picture I was seeing. It was Dallas Grant I was imagining. Desiring.

This is trouble, I thought. *This is madness.*

But I couldn't stop thinking about him. Once it was there, I couldn't get rid of it.

Before I'd even met him, I was hooked.

"Tell me it isn't true!" Amelia sobbed.
"Please, tell me it isn't true."
I had no idea what to say.

f o u r

My first meeting with Richard Showalter was a nightmare. Although with nightmares, you at least have the consolation of waking up.

We were having lunch at the Ivy, which was so cliché that it was almost exciting—it was my turn to be the one caught chatting over calamari. I could live with being A-list among the A-holes for an hour or so.

Richard was already waiting at the table when I arrived—promptness, I figured, was a good sign. He didn't stand when I got there, but he *did* hang up his cell and flash me a semi-genuine smile. He was as handsome as his photo had promised, and his body showed that he had a personal trainer who took his job very seriously. He was wearing a black T-shirt that probably cost more than a whole Old Navy store and Prada sunglasses that would keep the sun out but the shine on.

"Mallory," he said, looking at me as if I were his new girlfriend's more skeptical little sister. "I can't tell you how excited I am to be working with you."

We were sitting outside, and there was some sunlight

coming through the LA haze. Still, I wanted him to take his sunglasses off. I'd already learned to be suspicious of people who never showed their eyes; it was that hint of vampire blood.

"I've always been a big fan of your mother's," he continued, no fangs in evidence. "But I have a feeling I'm going to be an even bigger fan of yours."

Well, that was nice. At the very least, he'd done his homework.

I'd done mine, too—I knew that Richard Showalter had propelled himself up the production ladder by masterminding *Catfight*, a quasi-reality soap about four women in New York City who worked at the same fashion magazine by day, undermining each other every step of the way, only to hang out as best friends at night, frequenting the same upscale bar so they could talk about the guys they'd slept with. *Catfight* had been a huge hit one summer—spawning an otherwise inexplicable trend for drinking pink wine and calling men "disposable bedposts." But when Richard was snatched away to make a pilot for Fox called *Three Alarm Fire* (basically, *Catfight* with New York firefighters), the series became just one more *Entertainment Weekly* in-joke and was canceled for an advice show called *Is He Stupid or Just Plain Dumb?*

Three Alarm Fire was never made, and his future was never secured . . . until the *Likely Story* deal came along.

"I was a huge fan of *Catfight*," I said.

Richard laughed. "No you weren't."

"Well, in the beginning."

"You *hated* it."

"I never even saw it," I admitted.

"But you hated the very *concept* of it."

Well, this put me in a spot. Did I get more points for politeness or the truth?

I figured I'd opt for the truth.

"Yeah, it was pretty lame," I told him. "No offense."

"Shows how much you know!" he replied.

And this was before I'd even had a chance to order an iced tea. We were arguing.

"Excuse me?" I asked.

He smiled again. "This is only going to work, Mallory, if you admit that you're completely out of your depth and that you need my expertise. You don't know anything about running a TV show, and—I'll be honest—I find that refreshing. Usually I have to deal with creators who think they know everything, and that creates more messes than you'd ever believe. One of the great things about this setup is that you know your place and I know mine. If we get that down, the rest will be easy."

A few words popped into my mind, and they all rhymed with *ick.*

"There," he continued, signaling the waiter. "What will you have?"

I ordered without looking at the menu, to make him think I ate here all the time and was much more caught up in the scene than he ever would be. (He didn't have to know I'd researched it online the night before.)

Once the waiter left, Richard started talking about budgets and schedules and casting and keeping the network happy and making an "advertiser-friendly" show without "losing our edge." And I felt . . . well, I felt like he'd just called me an idiot and was now trying to prove it.

At one point, he asked, "Are you with me, Mallory?" And I thought, *Well, that's the question, isn't it?*

Was I with him?

Everyone—the network, Donald, Gina—was excited about him being the show runner. He seemed to know what he was doing.

But me. What about me?

"Yeah, I'm with you so far," I answered.

We were on much safer ground when we started talking about the story. Richard loved it. Loved, loved, loved it. Said I was a genius. Said he couldn't wait to read more and see where I was going with everything. He loved the friendship battles. He loved the romantic triangles and squares and hexagons. He loved how real it was. Despite myself, I grew happier. Because what writer can remain mad when an attractive, sure-of-himself guy makes a string of compliments that seem, even if they aren't heartfelt, at least mindfelt?

Next, we talked about casting.

"Isn't Dallas great?" Richard asked.

Cool as the inside of a refrigerator, I simply nodded.

"Apparently, we're not making much headway with his agent—she sees bigger and better things for him. Wants his launchpad to be some Minghella movie that might be made after he finishes his next three. But I think we're going to be able to cajole her into letting us fly him out here. Then, my dear, you're going to have to pitch like you've never pitched before. We need to hit the creativity angle to get him to sign."

This time I nodded with some difficulty. It was going to be up to *me* to pitch *Likely Story* to Dallas?

"About Sarah—" Richard resumed.

"I think I already found someone for Sarah," I interrupted. "This great actress. From my school. A real discovery."

I knew I had to downplay my connection to Amelia, so it wouldn't seem like I was just trying to do a friend a favor. Richard looked a little skeptical.

"Have her send a head shot to the casting director," he told me.

"Okeydokey," I replied. He had no idea what to do with that phrase. People in his world could barely spell *OK*.

For the rest of the lunch, we were unlike any other pair at the Ivy. We didn't gossip. We didn't flirt. We didn't look to the street for paparazzi. We just talked about work. A lot of work. I was exhausted by the end of it. Richard, if anything, seemed energized.

The reality of it all was setting in on me . . . and I felt the weight of it. All of the people whose jobs would be on the line. All of the money that was going to be spent. All of the sets that would be built. All of the ink that would be used to print out scripts. And the less tangible things, like the weight of expectations. The weight of chance. The weight of potential success. The weight of probable failure.

"This is going to be huge," Richard said as our lunch ended and he charged the check to the network. When he got up to leave, I realized that he and I were the same exact height—not what I expected.

"Huge," I echoed.

"Look," he said, pulling his valet check from his jacket,

"I'm not going to hold your hand. But I *am* going to watch your back. You have to trust me."

I hoped that I could.

I hoped he was strong enough to prevent the weight from crushing us both.

I didn't take comfort in everybody else's opinions.
They all had their motives.

f i v e

"What're you doing right now?"

Dates with Keith would usually start with this question.

"Nothing much."

Whatever I was doing, that would be my answer: "Nothing much." I could be saving a dozen little kittens from a burning orphanage, and if I saw Keith's number on my phone, I'd drop them in the flames to take the call.

As Amelia fretted about getting new head shots to send to the casting director, and as Mom seethed whenever she caught sight of me, and as I worked on completing the pilot script for *Likely Story*, Keith was the oasis. I'd sneak to the back door of California Pizza Kitchen, and he would smuggle me toppings. I'd hang out with him after school on Wednesdays, since that was the day he had off and Erika had therapy. We were free and clear, even if nothing felt free and nothing felt clear.

"What're you doing?" This time he was calling from outside a movie theater in Century City. If I jumped in my car, we could make a six o'clock show.

I looked at the scene I was writing on my laptop.

SARAH

Every time I think I'm ready
for the truth, I'm not.

RYAN

I never would have started
things with Jacqueline
if I'd known . . .

SARAH

Don't tell me, okay? Because
there's no way out of this.
You made a choice. Maybe
it wasn't the right choice,
but it's a choice we
both have to live with.

RYAN

But what if I didn't know
there was a choice?
What if I didn't know you
were an option?

SARAH

It's too late now. I wish you
hadn't told me. Any of it.

RYAN

But you're the one—

SARAH

```
     I'm the one you can't have.
     And you're the one I can't
     have. That's just the way
              it is.
```

This wasn't a transcription of any conversation I'd actually had with Keith. These kinds of conversations only happened in my head. I was just lucky that now I was going to be paid to let them out. If they couldn't be of any use to me, at least Sarah and Ryan would get something out of them.

"What do you say, Starbucks?" Keith asked on the other end of the phone.

"I'll be right there, Peet's," I replied.

I was such a sucker for all the classic things a girl isn't supposed to be a sucker for:

The dimples. The broad shoulders.

The unavailable boy.

There was still that nervousness at the movie theater, with both of us a little afraid that we'd bump into somebody Keith or Erika knew. To be on the safe side, we always played the role of "just friends" until the lights went down, and even then we kept it below the chair line. At first, it was thrilling—but like most thrills, that only lasted a short while. I knew Keith was tired of it, too; he wasn't afraid to tell me so, to wish out loud that things could be different. If only Erika wasn't so unstable. If only Erika didn't need him so much. In the darker moments, I wondered if maybe I was too stable, if maybe I should start to act more desperate. But why would Keith want two girls like that? Didn't I want to be the better one?

It used to be that I couldn't see a movie with him without mapping our story onto the plot. The killer could be delivering the head of the hero's girlfriend in a box and I'd think, *I wonder how Keith would react if someone beheaded me.* Stupid, stupid thoughts. This time I found another way to distract myself; as I watched the movie, I suddenly became the casting director of *Likely Story,* looking at each actor, no matter how small the part, and wondering if he'd be right for Ryan's dad or if she'd be right for Jacqueline. The answer was pretty much no across the board, but it was fun to speculate.

When the movie was over, the countdown to good-bye began. Most couples would go to dinner after a six o'clock movie, but Keith always had homework to do and a family (two little sisters) to get back to. He started asking me about how my writing was going—and then his phone rang. I could tell from the tune it was Erika.

This happened often enough. Sometimes he picked it up. Sometimes he didn't. At first, I treated all of these calls like they were tests. But every time Keith failed, I felt I was failing, too. So I stopped testing.

"Do you mind?" he asked. He always asked.

I shook my head.

"It'll just be a second." He answered. "Hey, Erika. . . . Yeah, just at the movies with Rob. . . . Rob from skiing, yeah. How are you? . . . Oh man . . . okay . . . okay . . . yeah, sure . . . no problem whatsoever. I'll be over in a few."

After he hung up, he turned to me. "Her dad freaked out again, and she and her mom are both a mess. It sounds like he totaled their car."

I told him to go. I thanked him for the movie. I said it was okay for him to leave. He was doing the right thing. I knew he was doing the right thing. It just happened that it wasn't the right thing for me.

I went to In-N-Out for a milkshake and some onion rings before heading home. Mom was waiting, claws out, as soon as I got in the door.

"Where have you been? I've been worried restless!" she cried.

It was phrases like this that made me think the *Good As Gold* writers hated my mother as much as they pretended to love her. They would give her these awkward catchphrases that no human being would ever say, and then have her repeat them from episode to episode. "I've been worried restless!" was one of the milder ones, used whenever Diamond got into trouble on the show (which was often enough).

Some of my other favorites?

"You make me want to baste my own heart in the juices of love!"

"I will not stand here and be treated like an arachnid!"

"The secrets I know could fill two Vaticans!"

"Money is everything . . . and *everything* is money."

I swore ("on the grave of everything that's good!") that the people in *Likely Story* would never speak like this. It was bad enough that my own mother did.

"You were out with that Kevin boy, weren't you?"

A few months ago, Mom demanded that her personal assistant read my diary and give her the highlights. I never heard the end of it.

"*Keith*, Mom. And, yes, we just saw a movie."

"I knew it! You're not being careful, are you? Why can't you listen? Now more than ever, you must not get pregnant!"

When I was six, Mom forced me to take riding lessons. They stopped soon after everyone realized that I enjoyed feeding the ponies carrots more than anything else. The only lasting thing I learned, which I used now, was my ability to cry out:

"WHOA!"

"They only want one thing," my mother continued. "They want power. And if they can't get that, they'll settle for sex."

"WHOA!"

I was not about to take relationship advice from a woman whose relationship to reality was remarkably questionable.

"If you screw up now," she went on, "I won't be the only one you're hurting. You have your own future now to think of, too."

"Is that what this whole thing is to you?" I shot back. "An insurance policy against me embarrassing you? Did I not have a future before? Do I only get one if I'm signed up to do a soap opera?"

This elicited a big diva sigh from Mom.

"You're impossible," she moaned. "Simply impossible."

"Somebody draw this woman a bubble bath!" I cried out. "Alert the masseuse! Having a daughter is just *too much work* for her."

Oh, how I hated her then, for making me act so hatefully.

This wasn't the way I talked to people. Only to her. Because it was the way she talked to me.

Her jaw was set, her eyes all cold fire.

"You forget . . . I'm all you have," she told me.

"And *I'm* all *you* have," I told her back.

I wanted someone—the maid, the gardener, a cat burglar—to walk in, to interrupt. But the house was empty except for us. We were, indeed, all we had.

"I have an early call tomorrow morning," Mom announced. Then she lifted her head and strode to her bedroom, leaving me standing two steps inside the front door, imagining the conversation we hadn't had.

Welcome home, dear. How was your day? How is your writing?

If you need any help, let me know.

For us, dialogue like that just wasn't believable. Because we were forced to write it ourselves, and we always got it wrong.

"I can't do this again," I said.
"I can only take so much."
"No," Keith told me, "you don't understand.
Something's happened. . . ."

six

The only break I got from writing the first script was when Dallas Grant was flown into town. Richard, Donald, and Trip were ironing out all the budgets and details that needed to be agreed upon before we shot the first episode. And Annie Prue, the casting director, was gathering head shots from all corners of the Hollywood universe, after sending out a description of each character (amusingly called a "breakdown"). Agents would send Annie all the photos, and then she and her staff would choose the hundred or so most promising actors and put them "on camera." They'd cull the best ones from those, and Richard and I would then take a look and choose some finalists to come in and read for us.

With Dallas, though, we were bypassing the usual process. Everyone felt he was the one for Ryan, assuming he knew how to act in front of a camera. We kept saying the show would make him big. But what we really meant was that he would make the show big.

I thought we'd just meet in the network offices, but that morning Richard called me with a change of plans.

"He's not the office type," he told me. "Even a studio office. I'll give him the tour, give him the dog and pony show, and maybe even throw a goldfish in if he likes goldfish. Trip'll dangle the moneybags, and I'll dazzle him with anecdotes from the *Catfight* set. But with you, it's got to seem real. We asked him where in LA he wanted to go, and he said the Getty. So you're going to the Getty. I'm sending a car to pick you up at noon. Be ready—I don't want him waiting."

I tried to sense nervousness in Richard's voice, but it's like he had all anxiety manicured out every morning.

The nervousness, I feared, was all mine.

"What will I wear? What will I wear? What *will I wear*?" I kept saying.

Amelia, who always cared more about clothes than I did, took this as a kind of victory.

"It's not like it's a *date*," she teased.

I was not going to dignify that insinuation with a response. Instead I said, "Look, everyone thinks he's the best. And he's the one you're going to be acting opposite when you're Sarah. So I'm doing this for you as much as for me."

"Uh-huh," Amelia replied. "You're not serious about those shoes, are you?"

It was 11:56 and I'd already tried on 1,156 outfits. It felt like my closet had made a suicide pact with my mental health.

"Just tell me what shoes to wear," I pleaded. "I won't argue. I won't resist. I'll do whatever you say. Just please end this hellish spectacle."

An hour. We'd been doing this for *an hour*. And it was hellish because I knew I had to look:

a) creative

b) smart

c) like I knew what I was doing

while at the same time I wanted to look

d) attractive

I had to pray that Amelia, who woke up every morning looking all of these things (especially the fourth), knew what she was doing.

I drew the line at makeup. Or at least I tried to draw the line at makeup. But Amelia wore me down. Finally, I agreed to makeup as long as it didn't look like I was wearing makeup.

"Whatever you say, *glamour girl*," Amelia teased. Then when I told her to stop, she changed it to *Mrs. Dallas Grant.*

"What is this, second grade?" I asked.

"Honey, I'll bet you *never* looked this good in second grade," Amelia countered.

Then she shoved me in my car before I could check out a mirror.

Immediately, I started biting my nails.

The Getty Center is the kind of place that Angelenos always say they mean to go but never do. As I took the tram up to the art museum, I was surrounded by foreign tourists talking in a full spectrum of languages. I tried hard not to study my reflection in the windows. *Either he's going to do it or he isn't,* I told myself. *You're not enough to influence it either way.*

When the tram got to the top of the Getty's hill, I let the

rest of the passengers leave before me. As I stepped out, I watched them disperse—going off in their own guidebook clusters, some to the left, some to the right, some swinging around to the gardens. The great thing about foreign tourists—even trendy ones—is that they rarely wear black. So I could watch their colors scatter—red in one direction, a pair of blues in another. Then I focused again and saw one figure moving against the tide, moving toward me. Coming closer. Recognizing me.

I had to blink. Once. Twice.

It was too unreal.

You know how in cartoons there's always a character who has a cloud following him? The rest of the sky can be blue, but this one character is always being rained on. Well, Dallas was the opposite of that. Wherever he was, no matter what the weather, it was like there was this patch of sunbeams that lit everything immediately around him.

This boy, I thought, *is a thing of beauty.*

And, even better, he was a slightly shy, slightly hesitant thing of beauty.

"Mallory?" he asked. A little—I swear to God—*bashful.*

"Dallas," I squeaked out.

With this confirmation, he smiled. His shoulders eased a little.

My chest tightened.

"Thanks for meeting me here," he said. "I know it's a hike."

"No," I said, trying to walk the fine line between babble and silence. "I love it here. It makes you think there might be a point to having rich people, if they all donate their art collections to the public like this."

"It boggles your mind, doesn't it?" Dallas said. "I mean, however many million years ago, a dinosaur dies. Eventually its body becomes oil. Some company comes along and pulls it from the earth. The owner of that company makes twelve million dollars and buys a Van Gogh. He builds a museum for it . . . and here we are."

"Yup," I said. "Here we are."

Cue: awkward silence.

Except: It seemed like I was the only one who found it awkward.

"So, tell me about this show of yours," he said, leading me down to the winding garden.

Don't you want to know about me first? I didn't ask. I had to remember: *This isn't a date.* There was no way this beautiful college student would ever be strolling on a date with a high schooler like me. This was business.

Head, your services are needed. Please leave the clouds.

Ultimately I reached a compromise with myself: As my mouth told him all about *Likely Story* and how groundbreaking and amazing it was going to be, my eyes got to catalog his features, doubling and tripling back to his eyes every now and then. I was telling him how my goal was to do something no soap opera had ever done before: namely, the truth. And the truth was that I was trying to figure out what color his eyes were, because they appeared to shift with each bud and blossom he looked at. Sapphire. Opal. Topaz. Agate. His eyes were every birthstone at once.

"What?" he asked.

I had no idea what I'd just said. He'd caught me staring.

"Your eyes are so many damn colors at once," I blurted out.

"I know. It's freaky, isn't it?"

Freaky wasn't the first word that came to mind.

"I'm sorry."

"What for?"

"Staring?"

Shut up shut up shut up.

I decided to change the subject.

"So, do you like Juilliard?"

He nodded. "It's fantastic. It opens so many possibilities."

I had a feeling he wasn't thinking of soap operas when he said that.

"What was the last play you did?" I asked.

"Chekhov. *The Three Sisters.*"

"Were you Andrei or Vershinin?"

Dallas stopped in his tracks.

"Do you know, you're the first person in all of Los Angeles who hasn't asked me which of the sisters I played?"

"My mother thinks Chekhov is a ballet dancer."

"So you've read the play?" he asked.

"I've typed it."

That wasn't the response he was expecting. "What do you mean?"

I couldn't think of any plausible explanation but the truth.

"This is so geeky," I said as a disclaimer. "But when I was in middle school, I went through this big playwright phase. I figured the way to learn to write like the masters would be to type out all their plays instead of just reading them. So I could hear them better in my head. So I would know what they felt like. To write. I know it's stupid—"

"It's not stupid."

"It was a lot of time I could've spent watching TV."

"I like it," he said.

"Thanks," I said.

And then we just hovered there, near the end of the garden.

"Hey," I said, "you never told me which of the roles you played."

It was so sweet—he blushed.

"Actually," he said, "it was a fringe production. So I played one of the sisters. Irina."

"There's more to you than meets the eye, isn't there?" I joked.

"God, I hope so," he replied.

I very well could have taken my heart from my chest and said, *Here, have this.*

Trouble.

We went into the galleries and floated from painting to painting. He studied them, and I studied him studying them. At least until I realized that most of the masterpieces were framed with reflective glass. He could see me hovering in each landscape, on every abstraction.

He spent a particularly long time in front of Van Gogh's *Irises.*

"It's amazing, isn't it?" I asked.

"It makes me feel inadequate," he said.

"Why?"

"Because don't you ever worry that you'll never be that good at anything?"

All the time. Including now.

When we were through with the art, we went back to the gift shop to have fifteen more minutes of talk before the studio cars came to take us away.

"Here's the thing," he told me. "I think your ideas are great. But they're asking me to sign a five-year contract. That pretty much blows my mind. Those are the five most important years of my career. I know a lot of people have gotten their start on soap operas—believe me, my agent has given me the full list. But do you understand, Mallory, what you're asking me?"

I did, and it made me nervous. How could anything I wrote be worthy of five years of his time?

"Here's what I think," I said. "More than any art form in the world right now, soap operas have the potential to become a part of their audiences' lives. Every day, five days a week, people tune in to watch a story unfold. Now, usually it's full of all sorts of wacko stuff and melodrama. But imagine if it was just like tuning in to the lives of a group of people you cared about? What if you connected with them so much that they told you a little bit more about your own life? I know it sounds ridiculous, and I can't believe I'm even talking about this as if it's, I dunno, *Dickens*. But there *is* an art to it. It *can* affect people, sometimes in a big way. I know your drama-school friends will probably tell you you're lame for doing it— although I'd bet they'd be jealous, too, that you'd have a steady job. I know the pace is killer and the demand is constant. And for all I know, my writing is going to be complete crap. But, man, if we do this right—it could be amazing. And it could reach more people in one episode than Chekhov's plays did in his lifetime."

With every sentence I spoke, my self-consciousness balloon inflated a little more, so that by the time I was done, it had taken up the whole gift shop and I had to shut up.

Dallas twinkled at me. I could tell he was still unsure, but at the very least he didn't think I was crazy.

"Plus," I added, "you can totally hit them up for mountains of money, because they *really* want you to do it."

"So *they* really want me to do it?" he said, leaning so close I could feel the air around his faint stubble. "What about you?"

I smiled, so completely nervous.

"Are you really going to make me say it?" I asked.

He nodded.

"Fine," I said. "I really want you to do it."

As we held there for a moment, in that teetering silence, I thought someone could have easily come in and painted a portrait of us.

Moment of Decision, it could have been called.

Or maybe just *The Start*.

seven

"How'd it go?" Keith asked me that night on the phone.

"I think he's going to do it," I said calmly, almost guiltily.

"How'd it go?" Donald asked me five minutes later.

"I think he's going to do it!" I said, not really believing it.

"How'd it go?" Amelia asked me five minutes after that.

"I THINK HE'S GOING TO DO IT!!!" I screamed, abandoning all self-control.

The next trick, of course, was to get Amelia cast as Sarah.

"I've seen the effect she has on guys," I told Richard the next day, digressing from a conversation we were having about my script. "She can't walk into a bar without some guy buying her a drink. Even if it's a salad bar. I swear."

"But that doesn't always translate into *acting*," Richard pointed out.

"It's even more intense when she's onstage. This one time, this guy got so infatuated with her when he saw her as the lead in her junior high school musical that he ran out and bought her flowers during intermission. *And she was playing Mary Poppins.*"

"I hate to point out," Richard said, not hating it at all, "that guys aren't really the gender we're trying to attract with a soap opera. With a side blessing to the gays, it's really the females we need to lure."

"But that's the thing!" I went on. "Girls should *hate* Amelia. But they don't! They *love* Amelia."

"Okay okay okay," Richard said, putting his palms up, relenting. "I'll talk to Annie Prue and make sure Amelia's on the short list. You have a pic?"

I pressed the first speed dial on my phone and a photo of Amelia grinning over an ice cream cone popped up. Richard took the phone out of my hand and had a long look.

"Not bad," he said.

From Richard, I figured this was pretty good.

There were definitely glamorous parts to the job—talking to reporters, visiting the studio, looking at Dallas's photo over and over and over.

And then there was the less glamorous part: the one that involved me at my laptop, typing away.

JACQUELINE
We're clear on this, right?
Ryan loves me . . . not you.
I've seen the way he
looks at you.

I've seen the way you look at
him. But I've also seen the
way he looks at me—and I know
what I know.

SARAH

I never meant to—

JACQUELINE

You never meant to <u>what</u>?

SARAH

I have no idea.

JACQUELINE

You have no idea?

SARAH

I mean, Mallory has no idea.
She just keeps typing. But
she has no idea what I should
say yet. All that she knows
is that in the next scene
Ryan is going to be getting
out of the pool.

JACQUELINE

<u>Another</u> shirtless scene for
Dallas?

SARAH

This time he's dripping wet.
I think she might even say,
"Rivulets of water course
down his chest."

JACQUELINE

Oh, honey, she's got it bad.

MALLORY

Excuse me? I'm right here. I
can read you.

SARAH

But, Mallory, what about the
boyfriend you already have?

JACQUELINE

He's not her boyfriend,
remember? He's still
with that crazy girl.

SARAH

Oh yeah. That sucks.

MALLORY

Stop it! I'm telling you, if
you don't stop,
you'll be wearing tracksuits

in this scene. <u>Orange</u>
tracksuits. XXL.

                SARAH
            (silence)

            JACQUELINE
            (silence)

                SARAH
            (silence)

            JACQUELINE
I'm just asking, how are you
supposed to know what we
should say when you don't
even know what <u>you're</u>
supposed to say?

            MALLORY
But giving other people words
is much easier!

                SARAH
So where were we?

            JACQUELINE
You never meant to <u>what</u>?

SARAH

I never meant to do anything
that could mess everything
else up. I never meant to
fall into something I had
no control over. And I never
meant for you to see that.

JACQUELINE

But don't you see . . . I
know you too well.

"Why is your name in there?"

I hadn't noticed Amelia creeping up behind me. She was supposed to be doing my Ethical Questions homework so I could finish my fourth draft of the pilot episode. Both the homework and the script were due the next morning.

"I think I may be going insane," I confessed.

"Well, in that case, you're in good company," Amelia comforted. "Hollywood is no place for the sane."

She went to her kitchen and came back with a bag of chocolate-covered pretzels.

"Brain food," she explained, handing the bag over.

"I hope my brain has an appetite," I said with a sigh. "I need it to be obese."

"I'm not letting you go to sleep 'til you're done!" Amelia warned.

"I'm a total fake," I told her. "Why did I ever think I could do this?"

"Mal, Mal, Mal-Mal, Mal." Amelia looked at me sweetly,

the sister I'd never had. "Don't you get it? Everyone feels like a fake. Everyone feels like they've gotten themselves into something they can't handle. Everyone's overwhelmed. That's just life. And here it's life times ten. Even if you feel like a fake, you just have to fake the best you can, and eventually you'll understand it isn't fake at all."

"Somebody's been reading a little too much O magazine," I mumbled. But really I felt better. Not that I was more confident in myself. But at least I had Amelia to be confident in me.

"You can do it," she said.

"Thanks," I replied.

"That's what friends are for."

And I thought, yeah, she was probably right. The thing was: I'd never really had friends like that. With all the moving. With all the school swapping. With all the cliques I hadn't mastered. With all the secrets I'd never learned. I'd never had a friend to show me what friends were for.

And now, I saw, I had just that.

It felt good.

I finished and e-mailed in the script at 7:59 in the morning. One minute early.

Such a pro.

Then I dragged myself through school.

Amelia had tried to stay up with me, but at about three I found myself talking to someone who'd fallen asleep on the floor, her face a centimeter away from the keyboard of her laptop. I tried to move her into her bed, but she just mumbled, "Here's fine" and went back to sleep.

When I got to school, Keith saw the state I was in and got

me a venti-sized iced coffee—a caffeine booster shot—with just the right amount of milk and sugar.

"You are my savior," I told him.

"All in a day's work, ma'am," he replied, tipping the brim of an invisible hat.

I gave him a blurry pre-caffeine kiss, then stumbled off to homeroom.

Normally, a coffee run on Keith's part would have made me giddy for the rest of the day. Amelia and I would have examined and cross-examined it: *What does it mean? Is he ready to dump Erika? He wouldn't get coffee for her, would he?*

Now it felt like old news. Or not even old news. Just news I already knew.

Richard had told me that Dallas was already on his way back to New York, returning to school while he waited for the casting process to really kick in. I imagined him walking his halls the same way I was walking mine. Did he feel a little different now than he did before? Would I cross his mind at all? I had no idea where Juilliard was in New York City or what it looked like. So instead I relied on my own imagination. I pictured ballet dancers practicing their moves on wooden railings set up in the hallways. I pictured drama students in black turtlenecks holding fake skulls and reciting *Hamlet*. I pictured both gayboys and straight girls turning their heads as Dallas passed by, completely oblivious to their involuntary attraction. He was smiling, thinking of our future together. . . .

On the show, I forced myself to add. *Our future together on the show.*

"Are you okay?" Scooter, a class-friend of mine, asked when he caught me daydreaming in Unified Sciences.

"Yeah," I told him. "Just writing in my head."

What I didn't tell him was that I was trying to write the future, not fiction.

Silly, silly me.

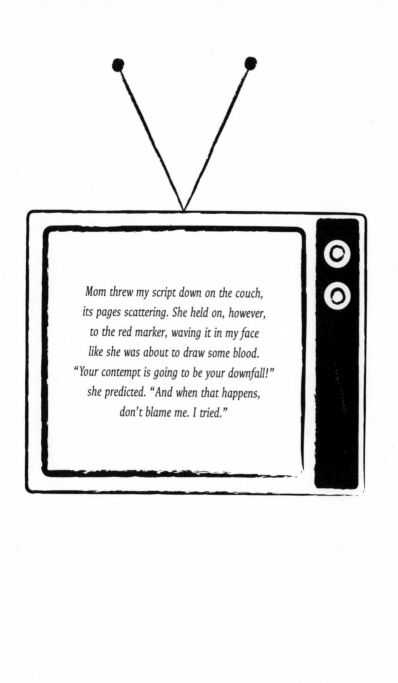

Mom threw my script down on the couch,
its pages scattering. She held on, however,
to the red marker, waving it in my face
like she was about to draw some blood.
"Your contempt is going to be your downfall!"
she predicted. "And when that happens,
don't blame me. I tried."

e i g h t

At lunch that day, I took out my cell phone and found three messages from Richard.

"Love the script," the first one said.

"The network's got it," the second one said.

"Can you skip school to get comments on Friday?" the third one asked.

Skip school? I would hop, skip, *and* jump it. It was starting to feel like I'd already left.

I called back and told him there wouldn't be a problem.

When I got home, I found my mom on the couch. But instead of watching her TiVo, she was entertaining herself in another way. She had my script in one hand. And a big red marker in the other.

"What are you doing?" I cried.

"Oh, just reading," Mom said, as if this was one of her favorite pastimes.

"How did you get that? You broke into my computer, didn't you? How dare you? That's my private—"

Mom held up a hand. "I did no such thing. You seem to have forgotten that you're working for *my* network. All I had to do was ask."

"Trip would never . . ."

Mom laughed. "Do you think Trip Carver makes xeroxes of his own scripts? What a stupid girl you can be. Rule number one of television, darling: Always get the secretaries very good gifts."

"That's not fair!" I protested. Then I walked over and put my hand out. "Give it to me. It's not meant for you to read."

"Too late!" Mom proclaimed cheerfully. "I'm already finished. And it's a good thing I did."

I knew I should have been walking away. I knew I should have been ignoring her. She had nothing to do with this. Her opinion didn't matter.

But, at the same time, I couldn't help myself. I cared what she thought.

"Why is it a good thing you did?" I asked. Even as it angered me that she'd made me ask.

She stood up, as if to give me support, although deep down I knew she was only doing it so I wouldn't be standing over her. Mom was all about the power dynamics.

"Sweetheart," she said sweetly, but without heart, "I don't want to see you get hurt."

"What is it, Mom?"

"You know how much I care about you."

"Mother!"

"It's a wonderful thing for someone your age."

"But . . ."

"But it's *horrible* daytime television. Absolutely wrong!"

I was not going to cry.

"How can you say that?" I asked.

She laughed again. "How can I say that? I think even you, Mallory, can admit that I have a head *full* of daytime television."

"*Likely Story* is meant to be different—"

"In daytime television, Mallory, 'different' is the same thing as 'difficult.' Kathy Smith doesn't want *different*. She doesn't want *difficult*. She wants something to divert her for an hour. She wants a little piece of story for her afternoon."

I was livid now. "Who's Kathy Smith?!?"

"Kathy Smith is thousands of women," my mother explained, although this first sentence hardly cleared things up. "Kathy Smith is the ideal *Good As Gold* viewer. I think about her often. I have a very clear picture of her in my head. If you don't think of Kathy Smith, then you are going to be a failure in daytime. Kathy Smith is the middlest woman in Middle America. She is in her early fifties and has been watching soap operas on and off since she was a teenager. She has children, but they're grown now. She has a job, but her hours aren't full-time. She loves her husband very much and has sex with him at least once a week, although she doesn't talk about it often. The truth is that she enjoys her time with the girls at the hair parlor as much as she does a roll in the hay. She knows when she turns on her television set at three o'clock that she will be able to catch up on a story that isn't her life, watching people whose problems are much worse than hers, whose lives are much louder than hers, and whose loves are much less reliable than hers. She may do other things while she watches—she may fold her laundry or pay some bills—but she knows these characters better than she knows her friends. Because she's been exposed to the intimate details of their lives on a daily basis for over thirty years."

As Mom talked about this woman, I could tell she actually believed that Kathy Smith existed, in the same way that so many of the Kathy Smiths believed that Geneva Sutcliffe existed. Kathy Smith was my mother's big fantasy, in the same way that Geneva Sutcliffe—and even my mom herself—was her fans' biggest fantasy.

And the worst thing was, I could tell that Mom *cared* about Kathy Smith. Deeply. Much more than she'd ever cared about me. Were something to happen to Kathy Smith, Mom would be distraught. And she wasn't even real.

Maybe for two seconds I was almost moved by my mother's allegiance to Kathy Smith.

Then I was pissed.

"I couldn't care less about Kathy Smith," I said. "She can watch your crappy show, for all I care."

Mom looked disgusted with me.

"How dare you!" she cried.

"I don't *want* Kathy Smith to watch my show!" I proclaimed. "Because if Kathy Smith watches my show, then Kathy Smith's daughter will *never* watch my show. Because Kathy Smith's daughter thinks Kathy Smith is the most boring woman who ever walked the face of the earth!"

Mom threw my script down on the couch, its pages scattering. She held on, however, to the red marker, waving it in my face like she was about to draw some blood.

"Your contempt is going to be your downfall!" she predicted. "And when that happens, don't blame me. I tried."

"Ha!"

"That's highly immature."

"Ha!"

"Stop that right now."

I couldn't help it.

"Ha!" I screamed out. "HA! HA! HA!"

You would think my mother would've had enough training in how to act when faced with a psycho in her living room. She'd certainly faced off against enough of them on *Good As Gold,* and those psychos usually had weapons. (My favorite was the one who tried to strangle her with a garden hose . . . *while it was turned on.*) But for all her melodramatic training, she couldn't figure out how to handle this one.

Finally, she said coldly, "Even if you don't care about Kathy Smith, I assure you that the network *does.* By the time they get through with your terrible script, you won't recognize it anymore. And I wouldn't be surprised if they turn the whole thing over to an *experienced* writer, one who knows his audience. I am going to write off your *hysterics* right now as a sign of how overwhelmed you are. And when this is all over, and you have given up this *adventure,* and you are crying because you thought you'd pulled it off when really, Mallory, you haven't—well, I will still be here for you, and we will put it all behind us, and I will pretend that this conversation never took place."

I loved how she put that—*I will pretend that this conversation never took place.* As if that would make it different from any other conversation we'd ever had.

"I'm just trying to help," she added.

"Smackdown is not an attractive parenting method," I

informed her, grabbing up the pages from the couch and storming to my room. The first thing I did when I got there was throw the script into the garbage can. Then I stared at it. And took the pages back out again. Only the first few were marked with red—it was like she gave up after that. Half the lines had Xs through them—I had to imagine that meant she didn't like them. Others had unkind comments in the margins—*Oh please* and *Wrong wrong wrong* and, once, *This isn't even writing.* I didn't think she would have shown them to me. But who knew? I was seeing her tap into deeper wells of nastiness than I'd ever encountered before. If she'd been able to divorce me, I was sure she would have.

There was only one star in the margins—the mark she always made when she particularly liked a line. It wasn't even a line of dialogue—it was a clothing description.

> SARAH glides in, her white dress
>   making her look like a swan.

Why that line? Was everything else so bad that that line stood out?

As a rule, I did not usually collapse on my bed in tears. But that afternoon, I did. Not because she'd yelled at me. Not because she'd torn apart my script. Not because she didn't love me.

No, this time I cried because I was afraid she was right.

I was a fake. I didn't know what I was doing. And I was about to be exposed.

"What are you doing?" Dallas asked, confused.
What answer could I possibly give him?
The truth wasn't an option. . . .
Or was it?

n i n e

I didn't take comfort in everybody else's opinions. They all had
their motives.

Richard wanted to get a show.

Donald wanted to get a commission.

Amelia wanted to get a part.

How could I trust them to tell me the script—the whole
idea—sucked?

The only hope I had was Dallas. He hadn't even read the
final script, just a first draft. And he'd been willing to commit
his career, his future, to it.

That has to mean something, I thought.

And then I thought, *Yeah—it could mean that he's as stupid
as I am.*

The hope-killers in my head had an answer to everything.

I could only hope that when Trip Carver fired me, he
wouldn't laugh in my face as well.

That Friday, I felt like a death-row inmate as I entered the
studio lot. After a quick call to make sure my mother wasn't

around, I decided to make a pit stop and get a hug from Gina.

"Oh, honey," she said as soon as she saw me, "you're a mess!"

From most people, I would have severely resented that remark. Because, let's face it, when you're a complete mess, the last thing you want from someone is a confirmation that you look like one. But with Gina it was different. She said it with such sympathy that I couldn't possibly be mad.

Suddenly it was all pouring out of me: my fears, my doubts, my fight with Mom, my certainty that I was going to be fired on the spot for being such a bad, immature writer.

"Honey," she said, "let me tell you a true story. When I first got out here, years and years and years ago, I didn't have a dime to my name. I'd worked at a beauty parlor in Brooklyn, and all the girls had told me to save up and go to Hollywood to be a beautician for the stars. Well, I did save up—but then I spent it all going across the country. A girl I'd gone to high school with had a college roommate whose older sister was going out with a guy who worked for the network. That was my big connection. But the day came, and I lugged in my whole makeup kit—it felt like it was the size of an army trunk! I gave these four actresses four different looks, and then I got the job. I celebrated, sure, but I was also sure they'd fire me on the first day.

"Instead, they asked me to do the makeup for Blanche Norwood. I'm sure you've heard of her—she was the matriarch of all matriarchs, the soap-opera actress all the women who are now soap-opera actresses grew up watching. Word on the street was that she was one tough customer. So I was petrified. This was when the soaps were still in black and white, so the makeup was all different; you couldn't rely on what it really looked like, but had to imagine what it would look like in black and white. And I had no idea. No idea whatsoever.

"So I get into her dressing room, and I'm afraid my hands are going to be shaking too much to do anything. I start taking deep breaths, calming myself down. I don't let any of this show while I'm doing her face. She looks at me every now and then, but mostly she's staring in the mirror, thinking about things. I'm imagining she's wondering which lover to go out with that night, or which person on the set to chew out. When I'm done, she doesn't even notice it. I have to say, 'Ma'am, I'm done.' And that's when she looks at me, and she looks at what I've done, and she looks back at me, and she says, 'Thank you. When we do our best, it all falls into place.'

"The first time, I didn't know what she meant. But each time I did her makeup, that's what she'd say when I was finished. I heard her say it to other people, too. And eventually I realized: She was talking to herself as much as she was talking to any of us. Maybe more.

"She was smarter than most women I've ever met, and certainly smarter than most men. So, honey, what I'm saying to you now is what she said to me then. *When we do our best, it all falls into place.* It might not be the place we're expecting, or even the place we want. But it works itself out. Because you know you've done your best. And people appreciate that."

She hugged me then. I didn't want her to let go.

"So you go in there and show 'em your best," she told me. "And if they don't like it, they'll have to answer to me!"

We met in a conference room right by Trip's office. Trip was there, and so was his assistant, Greg, who still looked a little uncomfortable that he had to wear a suit in order to take notes. Richard was there as well, chatting with Celene Thimble (VP of Daytime, who'd been at our first meeting), Holly Hughes (VP of Daytime Development—I had no idea what that meant), Webster Strong (VP of Daytime Strategy—an equally perplexing title), Frieda Weiner (pronounced "Whiner," Network Consultant for Daytime Brand Management), and Donnie Dixon (VP of something else—there were so many vice presidents it was sure to be a free-for-all when the president died).

Donald told me to go into the meeting with thick skin. Sadly, though, I seemed to have left my skin thickener at home.

Holly Hughes started off the meeting by saying, "Where are the adults?"

I explained that since we were going for a younger demographic, the emphasis was on the younger characters.

"Yes," she said, "but where are the adults?"

"At work or on vacation," I said. Joking.

Greg was the only one who laughed, and then he immediately tried to erase it by looking down at his notes.

The questions and statements started coming from all sides:

"What if the cast was Hispanic?"

"Can we add a set of twins?"

"There needs to be more drama. How do you feel about Jacqueline going blind? That worked really well on *Tomorrow I Love*."

"What if a hurricane hit Deception Pass in the second week?"

"I don't know that our advertisers really care about teenagers."

I had thought we'd be getting into *Can you change this line a little here?* or *Why not add a scene at the beach?* Small things. Not big things.

I kept looking at Richard for help, but he was nodding at everything that was said, taking his own notes with a silver Cross pen. And because no one would stop the tide of criticism, people kept adding more and more water to drown my script in.

"What if Sarah gets an STD?"

"Perhaps she starts sleeping with Ryan's brother, for revenge."

"What if she can read his mind? I mean, *really* read his mind?"

"Maybe she doesn't know who her father is!"

That last one came from Donnie Dixon, who then made it roughly a thousand times worse by looking at me and mumbling something about being sorry for saying that. Although deep down, I could *really* read his mind and imagine him thinking, *What the hell? At least being fatherless is something this girl knows about.*

I explained to them why I'd chosen to do what I'd chosen to do. I gave in to some points—sure, Sarah could have a dog—

and others I just pretended to take into consideration. What I really wanted to do was pull my script out of their hands and say it wasn't for them. But it was too late for that.

Trip remained silent the whole time, taking it all in. Finally, though, he leaned back in his chair in a way that made everyone fall silent.

"What do you think, Greg?" he asked.

Greg gulped, then made a point of looking me in the eye when he said, "I thought it was really good. Sure, you can change some small things. But at heart, it's really good. You can't mess with that."

Trip nodded, then said, "My thoughts exactly."

He then proceeded to say what we were going to do. I noticed a few of the comments had slipped into the grand plan—the word *adults* kept coming up—but, for the most part, I was safe. Trip liked it. He thought it was worth a risk. He wanted the VPs to "think outside the box"—and then said if the advertisers didn't like it, we could easily go back inside the box.

Our hour was almost up. Trip said Greg would type up the notes and get them to me by the end of the day; a revision was due on Monday.

I felt I'd been given a reprieve. And I'd learned something important: If you're going to get caught in a good-cop, bad-cop situation, it always helps to have the good cop be the most powerful person in the room.

After the meeting was done, I followed Richard to his car.

"Thanks for sticking up for me," I said.

His sunglasses were already on, and he wasn't about to take them off for me. So I could see my own reaction as he shot me down.

"This isn't a popularity contest," he told me. "It's a reality contest. You need to listen a little more and defend a little less, Mallory. Those people didn't get into those positions because they're idiots. Now, I'm not saying they have the best suggestions in the world—although I do have to say, I like the idea of a dog. But even if you're not going to do everything they tell you, you have to at least pretend you're going to think about it. And a lot of the time, you probably should think about it. Because as much as you think this is *art*, it's also business."

"Trip likes it," I said.

"Trip likes a lot of things," Richard warned. "And then one morning he wakes up and doesn't. He wants you to play the game, Mallory. So you have to play the game. That's the only way to get a show."

"So I have to add twins? Hispanic twins with a missing father and an STD?"

No joking around from Richard here.

"No," he said seriously. "But you'd better get used to the idea of some adults coming on board."

"But I don't like adults!" I protested.

"Adults never do," he replied. "That's part of the game."

After he drove off, I searched for Gina to tell her what had happened. But she was busy.

She has work to do, I reminded myself.

And then, with some fear, I reminded myself that I had work to do, too.

"Wish me luck!" Amelia said.
And I wondered: Why had that simple request
become so complicated?

t e n

They wanted an adult, so I added a bitchy mother character. It was lazy of me, I know—but I only had one weekend, so I had to rely on what I knew.

To balance her out, I also added a long-suffering husband, a caring but secretive doctor, and a few teachers who may or may not have been having affairs with one another.

I drew the line at shady arms dealers, though. My soap opera would *not* have shady arms dealers.

Scooter the soapfan was disappointed by this. We were having a brainstorming session during lunch period on Friday—although I have to say, I'm not sure our brains played a very big part in the storming.

"They don't have to be terrorists," he said. "Just shady arms dealers."

"How 'bout some shady tractor salesmen instead?" I suggested sarcastically. "That would break some new ground for daytime."

"Ultimately, there'd have to be a tractor accident,"

Scooter responded thoughtfully. "Maybe Ryan gets threshed and neither Sarah or Jacqueline can recognize him."

I sighed. "*Good As Gold* had a threshing disfigurement in the 1996 season. Remember? Rance thought he'd run over a scarecrow, but it was really Dominique."

"In Rance's defense, Dominique *was* dressed as a clown at the time."

"Only because she was trying to poison the grape juice at Rance's illegitimate daughter's birthday party!"

"Ooh!" Scooter perked up even higher. "I forgot that part!"

How many times had I explained to Scooter (and myself) that *Likely Story* wasn't going to be like these other soaps. We weren't going to have nun prostitutes, housewife ax murderers, or arsonist firefighters. But whenever we talked about plots, things like death by peroxide kept coming up.

"What if the arms dealer was a surgeon on the side!" Scooter exclaimed. "He could keep leaving the operating room to take calls from skeezy militaristic government officials."

I wasn't writing any of this down.

I knew I'd have to focus on writing over the weekend. Luckily, there weren't any big weekend plans for me to cancel in order to get my writing done. I was going to see Keith on Sunday because Saturday was Erika's, like our relationships had a custody arrangement.

Amelia wanted me to come out with her and some of her friends on Saturday night, but I used my revisions as an easy excuse not to go.

"Come on," Amelia said when I saw her after school on Friday. "It'll be fun! We're going to Ashley's, and I'm sure it'll be a wild time."

Amelia had all these friends that she'd been friends with long before I'd come along. She'd known Ashley since they were both in kindergarten. I knew I should've done more group things with them and gotten to know them better—but for some reason I never felt like we were on the same team. It's not that they were prettier or more popular than me—some of them were and some of them weren't. It's not that they had more money—at the very least, my mother kept up the illusion that we had plenty of money. But whenever I had a conversation with one of them, it felt like we were doing it for a reason other than the desire to talk to each other. Which made me feel awkward.

"I really, really have to get this done," I told Amelia for the thousandth time. "After all, you want your part to be as big as it can be, right?"

Amelia giggled. "Okay, I can go with that," she said. "How cool are you?"

I knew this was a question I wasn't supposed to answer.

Of course, on Saturday I only got through about two pages of revisions before my mind started to wander. I checked my phone a few times to see if Keith had called or texted—just in case Erika had canceled. But no luck. I forced myself to write a new scene with Sarah's new bitchy mother. Then I felt unfocused again.

Whoever decided to put a word-processing program on the same device as the Internet was one malevolent jerk. Because distraction is always a single click away.

I hadn't written in my blog since the night I'd ranted about soap operas. Almost every trade article about *Likely Story* had mentioned its origin, so I'd had more visitors in the subsequent days than I'd ever imagined I would get. There were 413 comments listed under my short entry—many of them from Mom's fans. Some, feeling motherly by association, cheered me on. Some were offended and called me ungrateful. Clearly, me saying soap operas were going the way of the dinosaur did not make the brontosaurus Kathy Smiths too happy.

As I scrolled through the comments, I realized I'd completely lost my anonymity. And I missed it. Now I'd have to think of total strangers reading what I wrote—each one of them a potential viewer for *Likely Story*. I never went out of my way to offend anyone, but now I *really* didn't want to offend anyone. I couldn't even start a new blog—the secret journal of an unnamed teenager who happened to be creating a soap opera. Because, I had to face it, there were no other people out there who fit my description. My life was a complete giveaway to my identity.

Finally, toward the end of the comments section, there was one from someone calling himself JuilliardSoaper2B. It read:

> Chekhov raises a glass to you. And
> Dickens sends regards.

I looked at the date: It had been posted the day after I'd been at the Getty with Dallas. He'd posted it the day he got back.

There was no e-mail address attached, no way to contact him. I was sure I could've tracked him down, but I didn't want to seem stalker-esque. So I simply posted a comment in return to his comment.

Van Gogh wanted me to say nice eyes.

Then I immediately deleted that and came up with:

Shakespeare's warned me that a show's
only as good as its cast.
I think we're off to a good start.

I figured the odds of him returning to my blog to see that were pretty slim. I would try to forget it was there.

Just before midnight, Keith called me.

"What're you doing right now?"

The honest response would've been: *I'm debating whether I'm actually allowed to use a certain four-letter word on daytime television or whether Sarah should just say her mother is full of crap.*

But instead I said, "Not much."

"Your mom home?"

"No, I think she's still out."

"Can I come over?"

Something about the way he said it made me pay attention.

"Is something wrong?" I asked.

"Yeah, Odie. I think there is."

"Well, Garfield, come on over. I'll meet you in the back-yard."

I knew it was a sign of some sort that I didn't immediately shower and change. But I couldn't figure out what my inaction meant—was I just so comfortable with Keith that I could let him see the real me, or was I giving up? Whatever the case, when I met Keith in the gazebo in our backyard, I was wearing my writing clothes—an old Decemberists T-shirt and torn jeans. Not exactly an *In Style* spread.

We usually met at the gazebo so I wouldn't have to worry about Mom seeing us. We were far enough away from the house, and the odds of Mom realizing I had stepped outside were slightly higher than the odds of me spontaneously com-busting. We were safe. And we could make all the "Sixteen Going on Seventeen" jokes we wanted.

"Hey, Ariel," he said when he got there.

"Hey, Jasmine," I said back. Then we kissed for a minute or two. Or three.

"Erika's asleep," he said when we finally came up for air. "At her house."

"Where else would she be asleep?" I asked.

And that's when he unloaded, telling me all about how Erika's father had flown into a rage the other night when Erika's mom had said she'd had enough, and now Erika's mom was trying to leave him, but he kept coming by, until finally Erika and her mom went to stay at a hotel until they could get some kind of restraining order. He'd never actually been vio-lent against them, but they were worried it had gotten to the point where that might happen. It was awful, and nobody really knew about it except Keith, and it was killing him. He figured it would be okay to tell me, since I didn't know any of them.

He needed me. That much was clear. He wanted to open up to me—and wasn't that what I'd wanted? Wasn't that what I thought relationships were about? He trusted me. He felt comfortable with me. He wanted me to help him find a way to help Erika.

And I just couldn't do it.

I felt selfish and wrong and heartless, but I just couldn't do it.

"I can't," I said. "I just can't."

"You can't what?" Keith asked, genuinely confused.

"I can't do this again," I said. "I can only take so much."

"No," Keith told me, "you don't understand. Something's happened. . . ."

"To Erika," I said. "Something's happened to Erika. Not *with* Erika. *To* Erika."

"I know this is weird—" Keith said, not for the first time in our "relationship."

"I want her to be okay," I interrupted. "You have to understand: I really want her to be okay. But every time I see you, it's starting to hurt me more than it makes me happy. You show up and one of the first things you do is tell me where she is so you can be with me. I feel like I'm aware of her every move. And I know she came first, and I know you care about me, and I know in some way it hurts you, too. But, Keith—I have a heart. You have to understand that."

"I know you do. . . . I know you do," he whispered, holding me close.

It had to stop. I knew it had to stop.

But I couldn't say those exact words. And that's what it would have taken: exact words.

"Let's talk about spaceships," he said.

"How about breakfast cereal?"

"Great mountain climbers of the mid-twentieth century?"

"Uses of the word *strumpet* in literature?"

We knew what each of us was really saying:

Anything but her. We'll talk about anything but her.

As if that could make her go away.

Instead all I could think about was him thinking about her.

"The show is a go," Trip Carver said.
"On one condition . . ."

eleven

Trip and all the VPs (and, hopefully, Greg) loved the revisions. In particular, they loved the new adults . . . so much, in fact, that they wanted even more adult characters.

"I'm going to draw the line somewhere," I told Richard.

"That's fine," he said. "Just make sure you draw it in pencil."

Scooter was more critical.

"Can't Sarah and Jacqueline secretly be sisters?" he asked.

"No."

"What if Jacqueline's real mom was blackmailed into giving her up? By a priest?"

"I'm not sure we need that, Scoot."

"Can babies have amnesia?"

"I don't think they remember much in the first place."

"Well, maybe Jacqueline has a repressed memory of being in the crib with Sarah, and Sarah stealing her silver rattle. Which is why she's trying so hard to steal Ryan now."

"The silver rattle is a nice touch. But no."

The good thing about Scooter was that he didn't mind that I thwarted his attempts at turning *Likely Story* into *Another Unlikely Story*.

"Do you have a crush on Ryan?" he asked me as our conversation came to an end. "Because you write like you do."

"Ryan isn't real," I reminded Scooter.

"Yeah," he said with a smile. "But your crush is."

After school that Tuesday, I had a meeting with Annie, the casting director, and Richard to go through the head shots that had made it to the final round. I was driven to the studio and was on my way to Richard's office when I turned a corner and ran almost smack into my mother.

I was about as thrilled to see her as I would have been to be rolling naked in poison ivy, but she didn't miss a beat. Trilling loudly for everyone to hear, she cried, "Well, look who's here!"

This was a classic Geneva line, meant to show her casual disregard of threatening situations. What does Geneva say when she sees a three-armed grave robber about to corner her into a conveniently open casket? "Well, look who's here!" Or when her homicidal stepson crashed through her bedroom with a flamethrower, intent on serving her medium rare? "Well, look who's here!" Even her third husband's return from a French POW camp was greeted with a "Well, look who's here!"—although that one at least was said with a catch in her voice and a Daytime Emmy–craving tear in her eye.

Needless to say, I felt more like the grave robber or the flame-loving stepspawn when she said it to me.

"Hi, Mom!" I said as cheerily as I could. Richard had now emerged in the hallway behind her, and I didn't want him to see me sweat. Ever.

"What brings you here?" she asked sweetly.

"Casting. You know how it is."

My mother, of course, didn't know how it was at all. The producers of *Good As Gold* were as likely to ask her to cast other parts as they were to ask her to fix the cameras when they broke.

"Lovely!" she cried. Then, digging deep into her past, to the script of *Danger at My Suburban Door,* a TV movie in which she played a housewife facing off against a murderously sexy handyman, she remembered something mothers were supposed to say: "Don't be late for dinner!"

"I wouldn't miss it!" I assured her.

We air-kissed, then went our separate ways.

"Bravo," Richard said, leaning in the doorway of his office.

"I'll give you ten bucks if you can prevent that from happening again," I offered.

"What—and miss the show? No deal."

He was extending his arm so that the doorway was blocked. This was not a casual lean.

I bent my head and ducked under his arm.

"Mallory!"

"Too late!"

I went straight for his desk, where there were printouts of ten logo designs. Two had the title right—*Likely Story.* But there were four other titles on display, each with two logo treatments. One was *Deception Pass.* I could almost understand that. But the other three sounded like they'd been crafted by a Harlequin Romance writer who'd been chained in a pink bathroom for two months with only a perfume bottle for sustenance.

For As Long As I Live

Love . . . Tomorrow

and my favorite,

Shadow's Light

"This doesn't make any sense," I said, holding up one of the logo boards. "Shadows *can't have light.*"

"You'd be surprised how well it did in the focus group," Richard said.

"What focus group?"

"We wanted to try out a few titles."

"Richard, the show's title is *Likely Story.* End of story."

"The focus group didn't get that."

"Who was in this focus group?"

"Soap watchers."

I smacked myself in the head. "Richard, have you been hearing me at all? This isn't for them. It's for their kids. And grandkids. And great-grandkids."

"I knew you were going to be like this," Richard huffed.

"What? Rational? Sorry if you don't agree. You can get your love . . . dot dot dot . . . tomorrow."

Luckily, Annie came by at that moment.

"You guys ready?" she asked.

"You're going to have to pick your battles," Richard warned me.

"Fine," I said. "I pick this one. Now let's go do some casting."

Annie was organized as ever, with the head shots in stacks for each character. At first I didn't see Amelia's head shot in the Sarah stack . . . but luckily that was just because it had gotten stuck to the photo above it.

"She's the one," I said. "She's the one I see in my head when I'm writing about Sarah."

"That's your friend, right?" Richard asked. Annie raised an eyebrow at this.

"She's really great," I replied.

"We want much more than 'really great,'" Richard countered, making me feel entirely lame.

Annie picked up the photo. "She does have the look," she judged. "It's nice to see a fresh face every now and then."

I restrained myself from cheering.

Annie put the photo back in the pile.

"We'll see," she said. "Now let's start with Jacqueline, shall we?"

After a while, looking at head shot after head shot after head shot can distort the way you see reality. You begin to realize how *weird* faces are. Especially smiling, blemishless, immaculately lit faces. It didn't take long in the casting process for me to start thinking about how truly strange it is that our head has three holes in the front and one on either side. The girls in the Jacqueline pile were almost all certifiably beautiful. But even beauty started to seem bizarre.

"Find anything?" Richard asked me.

I felt like I was down at the police station, looking at all the mug shots, trying to identify the right person. Only I wasn't trying to finger the guy who'd stolen my purse or the woman who'd held up the bank while I'd been waiting to use the ATM; no, I was searching through all the faces in order to find the one person who could bring my up-'til-now text-only character to life. With Dallas, it was easy: The plug fit the socket and the electricity just flowed. With Amelia, it was obvious. But with the other characters, it wasn't so easy. Part of me didn't want to let them out of my head. And part of me knew that if these characters were real, they'd never allow themselves to be posed for a head shot.

"They're all such . . . *actors*," I mumbled.

Annie pushed her silver bangs out of her eyes and said, "Yes . . . but if they're any good, you won't realize they are. It's our job to separate the wheat from the chaff."

She held up the head shot of a girl who looked like she'd been created in the laboratories of MTV to be the dim-witted blonde in a reality show called *Hot Tub*.

"Chaff," Annie proclaimed.

The next girl was posed in her head shot like she was waiting for her rapper boyfriend to toss her some bling.

"Chaff."

The next girl startled me. Her head shot actually looked . . . vulnerable. She was pretty, but she wasn't believing it.

Annie looked at me expectantly.

"Wheat?" I said.

She nodded. "Wheat. But don't get me wrong—if she wasn't attractive, she'd be chaff. We're in the attraction business here. Although sometimes *attractive* and *pretty* are not entirely the same thing. Some of the sexiest women this net-

120

work has ever seen have gaps in their teeth or asymmetrical cheekbones. Allure is elusive—but with the right eye, you can find it."

I picked up Amelia's photo and held it up.

"Wheat?" I asked.

Annie smiled and said coolly, "We shall see."

Word, it seemed, traveled faster than I did.

I hadn't called Amelia or picked up the phone because I wanted to tell her in person that she'd made the cut into the next round. But when I got to her house, she was already outside, jumping up and down. I half expected her to use her body to spell out the letters OMG.

"Thankyouthankyouthankyouthankyou!" she screamed as she hugged me. "Theycalledtheycalledtheycalled. Ohmygodohmygodohmygod."

"It wasn't just me," I told her. "Annie thought you had 'the look,' too. And Richard didn't, like, throw his body in front of her when she moved you to the callback pile—so that has to be a good sign."

"Pinch me!" Amelia said. "I mean, really. Go ahead. Pinch me."

The joke was, there wasn't really much on Amelia's bones to pinch. I managed to grab about a millimeter of her upper arm.

"Ouch!" she cried.

"Sorry," I said, stepping back. "You told me—"

"No worries. Assuming it doesn't bruise. . . ."

Amelia's concern was only momentary.

"I need to rehearse!" she said. "You need to help me."

We hadn't even gotten inside her house and already she was pulling me toward mine.

"Jake will drive us," she continued. "JAKE!"

Slowly her brother emerged from the house.

Amelia and Jake definitely had a smiler/smirker dynamic going on. If Amelia was the girl who grew up with puppy posters on her wall, Jake was the boy who liked to put puppies in the dryer for a spin.

"Your servant has arrived," he announced, barely looking at me.

"Shut up—you were going to Century City anyway," Amelia replied.

"I can't wait for you to be famous so you can get your own damn driver."

I sat in the backseat as they bickered for the whole ride. The stupid thing was, I almost envied it. I would've loved to have had brothers and sisters. Or at least one.

As we got close to my house, Jake said, "So I guess my sister's taking total advantage of your friendship, right?"

"That's not fair!" Amelia protested.

"Yeah," I said. "She didn't ask me to write the role for her."

"And I'm sure you're inviting all of the other girls who got callbacks for her role to come over to your house and practice with the script, right?" Jake snarked.

"Hey," I replied, "friendship has its privileges."

Once we had gotten out of the car and Jake had driven off to run over some old ladies, I thought that would be the end of the subject. But clearly some of Jake's shots had landed in Amelia's thoughts.

"You don't think I'm using you, do you?" she asked as we went inside. I knew my mother was on the set, so at least we didn't have to worry about her making a surprise guest appearance.

"You're not using me," I assured her.

"But I wouldn't have even known about the show if I wasn't friends with you."

I pinched her again, then looked her right in the eye.

"Amelia," I said, "we live in a connected world. None of this would have happened if I wasn't my mother's daughter. All of the other girls you're up against? They all have well-connected agents who no doubt got their own jobs because of their connections. But here's the thing: I have to believe that connections aren't enough. You also have to do good work."

"Unless you're Paris Hilton," Amelia said.

I nodded. "Unless you're Paris Hilton."

Amelia looked like she felt a little better.

"Are you ready to be Sarah?" I asked.

"I guess I was born for it," Amelia replied.

For the next four hours, we holed ourselves up in my room and read my pilot script aloud, with Amelia playing Sarah and me playing . . . well, everyone else. I was the most intense when we got to the moment when Ryan decisively pushes Sarah away.

                    RYAN
        Remember the first time we
                    met?

SARAH

Of course. Only guys forget
things like that.

RYAN

I've told you the story,
right?

SARAH

Well, I was there, too.

RYAN

But my side. You know my
side?

SARAH

You saw me across a crowded
room.

RYAN

Yes.

SARAH

And it took an hour for you
to come up to me and ask
what time it was. Even though
you were wearing a watch. And
then when I pointed it out,
you were so embarrassed you

almost ran away. But I
thought it was cute, so I
told you I'd give you the
time whenever you wanted.

                    RYAN
          Very romantic.

                    SARAH
          Yeah.

                    RYAN
          And a total lie.

                    SARAH
          What?

                    RYAN
     Well, I did see you across
   the crowded room. But it took
    me all of five seconds to go
      over to you. I'd tried to
    hook up with Jody Posner and
    she'd blown me off. I wanted
     an easier target, and I saw
      you just standing there.
       Completely alone. And I
     thought to myself, "Well,
        there's always her."

                    SARAH
          What? Why are you telling me
                     this?

                    RYAN
          I made sure my watch was
             outside my sleeve.
          Girls always fall for that.
          It was a total ploy.

                    SARAH
          You're lying. You just want
            me to stop being in love
                  with you.

                    RYAN
          It was a lie then. Not now.

                    SARAH
               Don't say that.

                    RYAN
          Truth hurts, doesn't it?

No matter how many times we read it, Amelia got all of
Sarah's emotions in her voice—that confusion, that pain, that
anger. She knows Ryan's lying (which he is), but the fact that
he's lying is as hurtful as the lies themselves.

She's good, I told myself.

But it was weird, too. Even though Amelia was saying

126

everything the right way, it wasn't the same as the Sarah in my head. It's hard to explain—it's not like I was picturing some other girl when I was writing Sarah. But I wasn't exactly picturing Amelia, either. It was just this voice. It didn't sound like me, but it was still mine in a way. It was like I was the actress, playing the part in my head. It was hard to expect anyone to match that. I couldn't even do it out loud.

"How was that?" Amelia kept asking me.

"You're great," I kept replying. And every time I did, she seemed so relieved. Not happy—just relieved.

I couldn't wait for the whole casting thing to be over. I had a feeling that I, too, would be relieved once Amelia had the part and we could both move on, together.

"Why can't human beings just act like human beings?" I asked Amelia. "I have an answer to that," she said.

twelve

The next step for Amelia was an in-person audition with Annie. She, Richard, and I had narrowed down the candidates for Sarah and Jacqueline to seven actresses each. Annie was going to make a quick trip to New York to tape readings with the actresses who lived there; the ones based in LA would come in to read for us at the studio. Apparently, actresses from the middle of the country would have to fly themselves to one of the coasts if they wanted a shot.

Normally I would have been out with Amelia in the waiting room, telling her to breathe and watching her stuff if she needed to go hyperventilate in the ladies' room. But this time I was already in the audition room, imagining her flipping through magazines like it was a doctor's office, looking at each page without really registering a word.

"Mallory, are you with us?" Richard asked.

We were in a conference room that was decorated with glass cases holding some awards the network's daytime shows had won over the years. There were some Daytime Emmys, but most of them, if you read closely, were for things like

Hairstyling in a Dramatic Series. *Good As Gold* had won for Outstanding Achievement in Live and Direct-to-Tape Sound Mixing for a Drama Series—twelve years ago.

I told myself I didn't care about awards. I just wanted to be popular.

"I'm with you," I told Richard, putting Amelia as far out of my mind as she could go. In this case "you" meant Richard, Annie, and two of Annie's assistants—one, Phil, who was going to read with the possible Sarahs, and one, Tracy, who was going to tape it for future reference. I wondered if that meant the network had archives for other actresses who'd started out on soap operas, like Meg Ryan or Amber Tamblyn. I figured I might be able to get some good blackmail for future guest appearances if that was true.

Annie went to get the first Sarah wannabe, whose name was Solstice Evans.

"Do you think her brother's named Equinox?" I asked Richard.

"Be nice," he warned me.

Solstice was clearly of the summer variety, tanner than a camel (and with bigger humps). She spoke fluent California, as if the end of every sentence had to go surfing. She was, I conceded, very pretty—but it was the kind of pretty that other girls wanted to kill. Not really how I pictured Sarah.

After Solstice read and we all thanked her, Annie went to retrieve the next auditioner, Alexis Randall. She was the one with the vulnerable-looking head shot that both Annie and I had deemed wheat. She was, I figured, Amelia's big competition. And for a few minutes, it seemed like maybe she hadn't shown up, since Annie was still outside, presumably looking for her. Finally Tracy left the room to see what was going on. When she returned, she was rolling her eyes.

"Looks like we have a stage mom in the waiting room," she reported.

Richard groaned. "God save us from the ones with mothers."

The issue, it seemed, was that Mrs. Randall insisted on seeing her daughter's audition. Annie was digging in her heels—she had a strict "no mothers, no agents" policy for the audition room. I was half hoping that the Randalls would storm out. But instead Annie and Alexis came in about a minute later, with Alexis looking about as embarrassed as a human being can get.

"I'm so sorry," she kept saying to Annie.

"It's okay," Annie said sympathetically. "Just wipe it all from your mind and show us what you've got."

Alexis nodded. Unlike Solstice, who'd dressed to inspire arousal, Alexis looked like she'd just come from school. When she looked at Annie or Richard, she seemed scared. But when she got to me, Tracy, and Phil, she seemed to be better.

She thinks I'm one of the assistants, I realized. And I was surprised that I was happy about that. I didn't want to be adding to her misery.

Phil gave her some pages from my script and explained how it would work. Alexis nodded, took a deep breath . . . and then became Sarah. Not the Sarah in my head, or even the Sarah that was written down. But her own Sarah, weak and defiant at the same time. She was the kind of girl who wanted something but had to dare herself in order to go after it. She was in love and hated the fact that she was in love. She wanted to be treated well, but put up with being treated badly in order to be close to the guy she loved. Alexis clearly understood that. Or she was just a really, really good actress.

"Thank you," Annie said when Alexis and Phil were done with the scene. I tried to hear approval or disappointment in her voice, but she was keeping it all hidden.

"You're welcome. Thank *you*," Alexis said, clearly wondering if there was anything else she could do. I was sure the first question she'd get when she returned to the waiting room was "How did it go?" I wanted to tell her she could say it went well, even if it was for a role that was already someone else's.

When Alexis was gone, Annie brought in Genna Sparks, who'd already acted in three soap operas. I knew her vaguely from the soap scene, and had been keeping track of her nose jobs as a matter of morbid curiosity. She had a twin sister, Audree, who must have gotten the same nose jobs at the same time, because no matter how much work was done, they always looked like twins.

"Hi, Richard," Genna said as soon as she walked in, kissing him on the cheek. Then she saw me and said hi. She leaned in, and I realized I was going to have to get some cheek action, too. At the very least, it let me take a look at the nose close up. I had to admit, her doctor was good.

Her reading? Less good. She sold the lines like she was a prostitute of prose, making every single NOUN sound like it was the dramatic CLIMAX for the whole SHOW. I wondered if SHE and HER FRIENDS always talked this WAY, or if SHE thought this was just what ACTING meant.

When she was done, she seemed pretty happy with herself. I suffered through a cheek-kiss good-bye and suffered even more when Richard said, "You were fabulous" to her before she left.

"Fabulous?" I asked while Annie went to get Amelia.

"Have you seen her on-screen? She's a natural."

"A natural *freak,* maybe," I mumbled. Tracy laughed. Richard didn't look amused.

I only dropped the subject because Amelia came in the room, looking majorly nervous. I hoped I was the only one who saw it, because I knew her so well.

Deep breath, I thought. And, sure enough, Amelia gifted herself with a big inhale/exhale, which seemed to balance her more.

She was on much firmer ground when it was time to read. We'd been practicing day and night, to the point that Amelia had pretty much memorized all the lines. Still, she had to pretend to be reading now, so Annie and Richard wouldn't think she'd had an unfair advantage. (An advantage? Sure. But unfair? I figured no, since she'd deserved to have it.)

It was strange to be watching her act out the lines instead of being the one to read them with her. I realized I couldn't really see Amelia as Sarah for the simple reason that I couldn't stop seeing her as Amelia. It was like when I saw my mother on *Good As Gold*—even though I knew she was playing a character, I never stopped being conscious of the fact that she was my mother.

When Amelia was done, Annie gave her the same "Thank you" she'd given all the other girls. I wanted to go over and give her a hug but didn't want to seem biased. So I just smiled, gave her an I'll-talk-to-you-later look, and let Annie walk her out.

The other three candidates for the Sarah role were in New York, so we moved on to Jacquelines. Only one of them—a girl named Stacy Chin—was impressive, but even she didn't blow me away.

"Maybe Alexis would be good for Jacqueline," I said as soon as the last actress had left.

Annie held up her hand. "No talking about it yet, okay? I don't want any minds to be made up until we see the New York girls. Otherwise, their agents will have my head."

Still, even Annie's order couldn't keep Richard and me from swapping notes on the elevator ride back down to the lobby (where I knew Amelia would be waiting for me).

"Wasn't Amelia great?" I asked, making it clear what I thought.

"For a beginner, sure," Richard replied.

"Well, the whole point of this show is to bring new blood to daytime," I pointed out.

"Ratings would be nice, too."

"And I expect you think *Genna* can get you ratings?"

"Perhaps."

"She's a good cheek kisser, I'll give you that."

Richard gave me an icy stare. "You know, Mallory," he said, "some girls can pull off being attractive when they're bitchy. You're not one of them."

With that, the elevator doors opened. I saw Amelia on one of the lobby lounges, and I didn't want her to hear this conversation.

"Have a nice night, Richard," I said.

"Oh, you too," he said back, as sincere as a six-year-old forced by a teacher to apologize to the girl he's been teasing.

I knew it was important to tell Amelia how great she was before she had to ask, but I still couldn't help muttering about Richard once he was gone and I was safe.

"Why can't human beings just act like human beings?" I asked Amelia.

"I have an answer to that," she said.

"And what's your answer to that?"

"Shopping," she replied. "Whenever you're in the position to ask that question, it's time to go shopping."

How could I disagree?

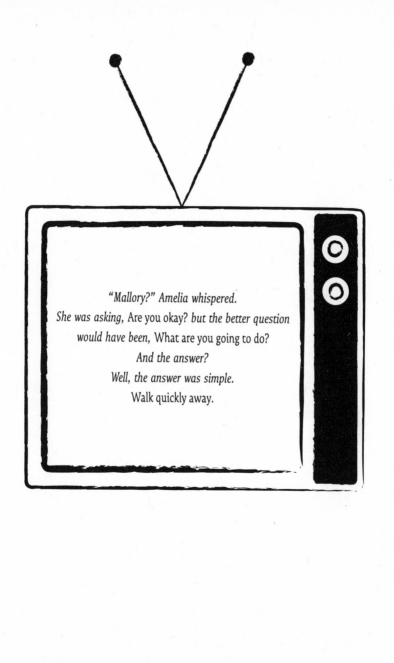

"Mallory?" Amelia whispered.
She was asking, Are you okay? *but the better question
would have been,* What are you going to do?
And the answer?
Well, the answer was simple.
Walk quickly away.

t h i r t e e n

I knew it was a school night, but luckily I got my mother's voice mail, so I could tell her I was heading to the Beverly Center instead of asking her. Amelia tried to convince Jake to drive us, but he was close to a high score on something, so we cabbed it instead. Having an income made it so much easier to justify cab fare. Plus, I assured Amelia, her audition had gone so well that it was looking like we'd both be paid by the network before too long.

The Beverly Center was the place Amelia and I went to shop when we didn't really want to buy anything. It wasn't as cool as the boutiques in West Hollywood or even as mall-satisfying as the stores in Century City. But it did give us an opportunity to do some seriously engrossing people watching and to try on sale clothes at Neiman Marcus in an effort to outdo each other in sheer hideousness.

We headed into the permafrost air-conditioning, and a more primal urge than shopping took hold.

"I'm so hungry I could eat that handbag," Amelia said, gesturing toward Coach.

"I'm seriously considering that saleslady, too. Pearls and all," I replied.

"Sbarro or Quiznos?"

"Really, that's just a choice between mozzarella or cheddar."

"So what'll it be?"

"Which is closer?"

"Quiznos, I think."

"Well, it's fated, then."

Arm in arm, we strolled down the corridor, making rude puns about sour cream and salsa. Because we were arm in arm, I nearly got whiplash when Amelia stopped short.

"What?" I asked, figuring she'd spotted a sale.

She hesitated for a second—and that was what made me look. Straight ahead, right outside Diesel, was Keith.

And Erika.

My arm dropped out of Amelia's. It was so funny—I'd spent all this time worrying that Erika would run into Keith and me that it had never occurred to me that I might run into the two of them. I'd seen pictures of her—you couldn't be in Keith's room without seeing plenty of pictures of her—and I'd even, early on, followed him once after he said good-bye to me to meet up with her. But that, at least, had been expected. This was like a punch in the gut.

Her hair was really short, in that way that looked like she'd cut it herself. But her face could take it—there was something very doe-like about her, from the big-but-not-too-big eyes to the cheekbones to the smallish mouth. I felt like a moose in comparison, even if that wasn't entirely fair.

They weren't talking, but his arm was around her. It didn't

look like they were about to make out or anything—more like they were about to spend the rest of their lives together. They were a pair. Anyone who saw them would know they were a pair.

"Mallory?" Amelia whispered.

She was asking, *Are you okay?* but the better question would have been, *What are you going to do?*

And the answer?

Well, the answer was simple.

Walk quickly away.

But I had to look for a second longer. Two seconds longer.

I had to see why Keith and I were never going to be together.

Lately I'd been picturing Erika as this frail, helpless girl. But I realized now that was only the picture Keith wanted me to see.

They were turning now, walking away from us. But even from behind, I could see how close they were. Even after he put his arm down. Even though they still didn't talk.

"Oh, Mallory," Amelia said, full of sad sympathy, now that they were going, now that they were almost gone. I wanted to tell her I was okay. I wanted to tell her I was devastated. I wanted to tell her I was angry.

But all I felt was hollow. This complete emptiness. I envied the women in soap operas, who would have no doubt fainted at the sight. Or screamed. Or fainted while screaming. A character in *Good As Gold* wouldn't just keep heading to Quiznos.

"I don't know why I'm so bothered," I told Amelia. "I mean, I knew this was happening. She *is* his girlfriend. I've never been."

Amelia didn't argue, which I appreciated. She didn't say, *Dump that jerk* or *You're so much better than she is* or *You deserve better*—if I wasn't going to dramatize the moment, she wasn't going to, either.

It wasn't until we were sitting at the food court over trays of subs and sodas that Amelia said, "Maybe it's a sign."

I shook my head. "It's not a sign. A sign represents something else. This was exactly what it was."

I couldn't accuse Keith of being dishonest; he was always honest with me. Sometimes painfully so. He'd never hid the fact of Erika from me; he'd just left its meaning ambiguous. I'd known he had a girlfriend when I first kissed him. He'd told me. I'd kissed him anyway. Wasn't this what I deserved, then?

The whole time we ate, I kept my eye on the crowds. Waiting for the two of them to reappear. Preparing to ignore them if I had to. Knowing if Keith showed up, I'd have to let him walk by. I would have to make myself invisible. Which wouldn't have been too hard . . . since it was exactly how I felt.

There was no question about it:
I'd been betrayed.

f o u r t e e n

My self-imposed invisibility continued the next day at school. Keith texted me a few times and wanted to meet up, but I made excuses. I told him I was busy, even when the only things busying me were my rapid-fire thoughts.

Scooter saw I was gloomy and tried to brighten things up.

"Maybe Ryan is carjacked, and when he manages to pull off the carjacker's ski mask, he finds out . . . it's his own grandmother!" he whispered to me between first and second periods.

"Or Jacqueline can hit her head on a rock and spend a month thinking she's a fairy named Gaiety" was the suggestion between third and fourth.

Lunch brought "Surely someone had to be handcuffed to the steering wheel of a runaway go-kart?"

Then, between sixth and seventh, "I know alien abduction's been done, but what if the whole town is abducted by *illegal aliens*?"

"Scooter," I had to tell him, "if you're trying to distract

someone, usually you try to do it in the direction *away from* what she's thinking about."

"Good point," he said. "Unless that distraction happens to be a blimp armed with an explosive device that's about to devastate the Deception Pass prom!"

When Scooter wasn't plot-twisting me, it was like I slipped into a waiting time. Waiting for Annie to return from New York with the rest of the audition tapes. Waiting for the latest round of comments on my script. Waiting for Amelia to get the job, for production of the pilot to actually start, for Dallas to fly back to California.

Most of all, though, I was waiting to figure out what to do with Keith. As if the answer could come from somewhere outside of me. As if it wasn't my decision at all.

To make matters worse, Mom had a week off from work. This meant she had time to make "appearances"—at local shopping-mall openings, at soapfan conventions, at low-level movie premieres. And even, every now and then, at our house.

I tried to stay in my room, writing. But I guess this hiding place was too obvious, since she found me there every time.

That Saturday night, at around midnight, she stood in my doorway and watched me typing away.

"You look horrible," she said.

This was her twisted way of showing concern.

"It's been a long week," I told her.

She angled to read what was on the screen. I blocked her.

"Fine," she said.

"It's not final," I told her. "I haven't even read it through myself."

"Oh, you writers! I remember your—" She stopped. It wasn't like her to stop in the middle of a story.

"My what?"

"It's nothing."

It occurred to me then.

"Were you about to say *father*? *Your father?*"

Mom looked genuinely surprised.

"No, I was not about to say *your father*. What a silly thing to assume. I was about to say *I remember your first novel*. Do you remember it?"

I shook my head.

She continued, "You were in first grade. You came home from school and said, 'I've written a novel.' When I got home from work, the maid told me this, and I went straight to your room and asked if I could read it. At first, you didn't want me to. You said nobody at school had read it, not even Mr. Morris. I told you I would be honored to be your first reader. Then you reached under your pillow—it was under your pillow—and handed it over to me. It was three pages long. Do you remember what it was called?"

And the strange thing was, I *could* remember it now.

"*The Cat Is Bad*," I said.

Mom smiled wistfully and nodded. "Yes, *The Cat Is Bad*. If I remember correctly, it was about a cat named Cat that kept hitting people. Until it met a dog named Rufus, which I believe you spelled with a *ph*. I don't think you said as much, but I believe they fell in love. The end."

"The end," I repeated.

We just sat there for a moment. I stopped blocking the screen, but she didn't look at it.

"I wonder where I put that story," she said finally. "I'm sure the PR department would love to see it." She stood up and patted the back of my chair. "Don't stay up too late. Even writers need their sleep. It's the nectarine of life."

"Nectar, Mom. It's the *nectar* of life." I couldn't believe I was correcting her clichés.

"That's what I said. Now get some shut-eye."

I promised I would. Then I stayed up another four hours, trying to figure out Sarah's and Ryan's and Jacqueline's lives since I couldn't figure out my own.

At about four in the morning, I heard Mom walking around, filling the house with insomniac noise: tiny, restless steps and quiet, unhappy movements. Usually she slept well—perhaps the only person in Hollywood who did so without the help of pills.

I wondered what was keeping her up now, but wasn't about to ask.

That was my own way of expressing concern.

Once Mom jetted off on her weeklong soap junket, things settled down a little—if *settled down* can mean daily meetings with your executive producer. Every day, a studio car would pick me up after school and take me to meet with Richard as we put *Likely Story* together. (Luckily, Donald had snuck title approval into my contract, so *Likely Story* stayed *Likely Story* and didn't become *Shadow's Light* or *Evil's Good Points* or *Hate's Love* or *Stupidity . . . Today.*) The studio car was just a plain Lincoln Continental, but from the way some people in my school reacted, you would have thought it was a stretch limo. I could see the popular girls shoot me resentful looks, barely containing their envy. Scooter was so excited about it that I started giving him a ride home . . . until Richard chided me for being late. I did not enjoy being chided. Which made it hard to work with a chider.

I think Richard expected me to be overwhelmed by all of the things that needed to be done. Luckily, growing up on a soap-opera set had prepared me to be at least familiar with all of the things that went into putting a show together. Most of the things—scenery, sound editing, boom operating, catering— were ones I wasn't going to get involved in; I freely admitted to Richard that I knew as much about sound editing as I knew about how a plasma screen actually worked. I was happy just to press the power button and let other people worry about how the picture got there.

It was the creative decisions—like casting and set design— that I wanted to be involved in. Annie was returning on Tuesday with the casting material, which left Monday for Richard and me to concentrate on all the inanimate objects. Together, we looked over the set designer's models. It was so strange to see Deception Pass coming to life—suddenly Sarah had a bedroom and Jacqueline's house had a living room. I felt like I *recognized* them, and at first I wondered how the set designer had managed to sketch out something that had existed in my head. Then I realized that I *did* recognize the sets—and not from any creative space deep inside my mind. I recognized them because I'd been seeing them my whole life.

"Don't these look a lot like the *Good As Gold* sets?" I asked.

"What are you talking about?" Richard replied with his customary care. "These look nothing like *Good As Gold*."

"Not the actual furniture. Or the colors. But the sets. That bedroom looks like Diamond's bedroom—the windows and the door and even the bed are in the same place. And that living room has the same exact dimensions as the one in the Netherlander mansion. I think the couch is the same couch."

"It's not the same couch."

"It *is* the same couch. I've played hide-and-seek behind that couch for as long as I can remember. I *know* that couch. Can't we get a lime-green couch or something different?"

I didn't know why I was being so insistent. But I sensed there was something Richard wasn't telling me.

"Look," he said, "if you want me to ask Monica to change it up, we can change it up. But you have to understand that sets are pretty much all set up the same way. You need to give the cameras room to maneuver in, and that limits your options. If you want to be innovative with your writing, go for it. But we can't be too innovative when it comes to the couches."

"Okay, Mr. Sunshine," I replied. "I was just making a simple point. I'm not asking for all the beds to be converted into bunk beds."

He grunted at that and kept looking at the sketches.

I wondered what Richard was like at home. I could picture it as one of those places in a style magazine—pathologically tidy, everything matching, each shirt evenly spaced out in the closet.

I couldn't picture anyone else living there with him.

"Do you have a girlfriend?" I asked now.

Richard didn't even look up as he said no.

"A boyfriend?"

Again, eyes on the sketches and "No."

"A dog?"

Now he looked at me.

"A show," he said. "That's what I have, Mallory. A show."

He shuffled some of the sketches around.

"I guess I have a show, too," I said.

He didn't even nod.

"Well," I said, "I still wouldn't mind a frickin' boyfriend."

That made him smile. Then he asked me if I thought Jacqueline would prefer drapes or shades in her bedroom.

There were important decisions to be made.

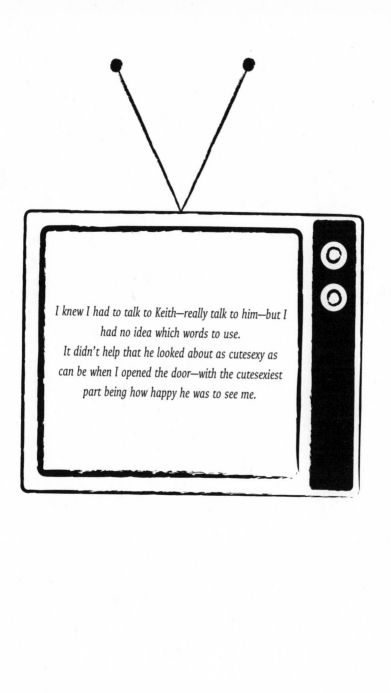

I knew I had to talk to Keith—really talk to him—but I had no idea which words to use.
It didn't help that he looked about as cutesexy as can be when I opened the door—with the cutesexiest part being how happy he was to see me.

f i f t e e n

Francesca Moore.

Annie brought back many casting videos from New York, but most of all she brought us Francesca Moore.

Her name was the first thing off Annie's lips when we met that Tuesday.

"Francesca Moore. If she isn't a star, then I'm going to retire and take up pottery."

It got worse: Francesca Moore was a classmate of Dallas's at Juilliard. He had recommended her.

"Are they friends?" I asked Annie.

"Why, I didn't ask," she replied.

Then it got even worse: Her audition video was fantastic.

"She's Jacqueline," I said when it was all over.

"Not Sarah?" Richard asked.

"No. Jacqueline. She's exactly how I picture Jacqueline."

"So who's Sarah?"

"I told you—it's Amelia. It's been Amelia all along."

"What about Alexis?" Annie asked.

"Or Genna?" Richard chimed in.

I looked at Annie's assistants Phil and Tracy.

"Help!" I said.

"I could see her as Jacqueline," Phil said.

"This," Tracy said, "is why we have another round to go."

Sure enough, this took the pressure off. We narrowed it down to five actresses—Amelia, Francesca, Alexis, Genna, and Stacy (who'd auditioned for Jacqueline's role)—and decided to have them read for both of the lead female parts.

"We'll get the contracts out tomorrow, and hopefully we can fly Dallas in for the scenes next week," Annie said.

Dallas. Next week.

The enormity of everything was hitting me like, well, *enormity.*

Richard brought the audition tapes to the VPs for our next meeting.

"I really like Amelia for Sarah," I said.

Everybody looked at me, not caring very much. I realized this was probably the wrong moment to speak up.

"We'll see how the next round goes," Trip Carver said. "We're still finalizing *all* the casting."

Something about the way he said it made me wonder if there was other casting going on that I didn't know about.

After the meeting, when we were safely back in our temporary production office, I talked to Richard about it.

"I thought we were casting Sarah, Jacqueline, and Ryan first," I said. "Right?"

"Yeah yeah yeah," he replied. "That's the plan. But we still have to look at the bigger picture."

I didn't like the sound of that.

"What bigger picture?" I asked.

"Mallory, you have to be ready to compromise."

I *really* didn't like the sound of that.

"Compromise about *what*, Richard?"

"Have you been listening in these meetings?"

"Yes," I said, annoyed that he thought I wasn't listening. "We talk endlessly about demographics and advertisers and how to sell the show. I'm aware of all that."

"Then you realize they want the show to skew older. To adults."

I shook my head. "That's not the plan. The reason they agreed to do this in the first place was so they could get a younger demographic. Teens don't watch soaps anymore. This will get them to watch. It's the anti–*Good As Gold*. It's *Bad As Basalt*."

"Basalt?"

"It's a rock."

"If you say so."

"I do say so."

"Basalt aside, Mallory . . . you say you want it to be radically different, but it can't be radically different."

"Why not?" I challenged.

"Because *there aren't enough teenagers at home after school to give us high ratings.* That's the reality, Mallory. You're a teenager—you should know this. What are most teens doing at three o'clock? Are they at home watching TV? No! They're playing sports. Or rehearsing for the school play. Or working at the mall."

"They can record it and watch it later."

"And how often do you do that, Mallory?"

"So you're saying we need to appeal to adults, too."

"It's inevitable."

"But adults will watch something about teens."

"Absolutely. That's why we're doing this. You're right about one thing—we don't want to end up like *Good As Gold*."

Something about the way he said this made me feel defensive. Not even for my mother. For Gina, really, and everyone else I'd grown up around.

"How many changes am I going to have to make?" I asked Richard.

"Some."

"You've talked to them without me there?"

"What do you think I do during the day? Wait for you to show up?"

"There are some things I won't do."

"Like what?"

"I don't know yet," I answered honestly. "But I'll know when you ask me to do them."

"Compromise, Mallory. It's all about compromise."

"Do you know how patronizing you sound when you say that?"

This time Richard actually put his hand on my shoulder. Not gently.

"You have to realize," he said, "these people *are* our patrons. *I* am your patron. We are allowed to be patronizing. We have the money, and we're the ones who lose it if this fails. Know your place and you'll be fine."

"Is that a threat?"

"Don't be so melodramatic. It's a warning, not a threat.

Patrons aren't the enemy, Mallory. They're actually your biggest supporters."

"Thanks," I said, not meaning it at all. "I feel a lot better."

We got back to work, but my heart was nowhere near it. I kept hearing the same words over and over: *Know your place and you'll be fine.*

I felt I knew my place, all right.

And it pretty much sucked.

I knew that even when my mom was away, Gina still had to work. After I was done with Richard, I sat in the parking lot and leaned against one of the back wheels of her car, waiting for her to come out from the studio.

She didn't seem surprised to see me—just like she never seemed surprised to see me hiding in the backseat when I was younger. But she did look concerned.

"What is it, honey? Rough day?"

"Is it always this hard to be a grown-up?" I asked.

Even though she was wearing her nice work clothes, she sat down next to me and leaned against the car.

"Yes, it is," she said. "Especially when part of you is still a kid."

"I thought I knew what pressure was before," I confessed to her. "But this makes the SATs look like a book report on *Goodnight Moon.*"

Gina put her arm around me, and I could smell her perfume. That scent might as well have been called Comfort—ever since I was a little girl, that's what it meant to me. It couldn't protect me from the nighttime fears, when I was home alone with my mother. But it could definitely help me with all the daylight worries.

"You're always here," I told her now.

"That's right," she said, squeezing me a little closer. "Sometimes it's not that complicated. Sometimes you just know what to do and you do it."

"But what if I'm wrong?"

"Then you're wrong, and you admit it, and you make it right. Look, it's not usual for a girl your age to have a job like this. It's wonderful that you have the opportunity. But you can't take it home with you. You can't let it run your life. That's what your mother, bless her, does. She made her choices, and I'm not saying they were the wrong ones for her. But you have so much ahead of you. You can't let these things get to you."

This might have been the closest Gina had ever come to saying something negative about my mother in my presence. But somehow she did it so that she seemed loyal to both of us at the same time. I wouldn't have known that was possible.

"Do you want to come home for dinner?" she asked me now.

"Yeah," I said. "I'd like that."

Here I was, caught up in the make-believe world that I was making. But really what I wanted most of all was a home-cooked meal and the believing that could come of that. For a few hours, I wanted everything to be real. Then I could return to my life.

"Guess who I saw the other day," I said.
"Elvis?"
"No, Keith. I saw you and Erika."

s i x t e e n

I couldn't avoid Keith forever (a) because we went to the same school and walked the same hallways and (b) because after the initial shock wore off, I didn't want to.

In this equation, the first reason pretty much ensured that we'd run into each other, and the second reason made me feel stupid. My anger was subsiding because I didn't have enough kindling to fuel it. The old sense of missing him started to kick in, and I couldn't kick it away.

Most guys, I knew, would stop calling and texting after a few days. But not Keith. More than two weeks after I'd seen him and Erika at the mall, he was still trying to get together. Granted, if he'd known I'd caught him, it might be a different story. But what, really, had I caught him doing? It's not like he'd lied; he'd been straightforward about Erika all along. It just meant something different now that I'd seen it. But that wasn't his fault.

"I should talk to him," I kept telling Amelia.

Finally, that Friday, she relented and said, "Go ahead. Talk to him."

"You think it'll be a disaster?" I said.

"No more than if you keep going like this. Just do it. Because not doing it is going to drive both of us crazy."

Amelia tried hard to sound mad at me, but it was pretty hard for her to do. Annie had messengered the contract over to her house, and her lawyer was looking it over even as we spoke. The network didn't want to leave anything to chance—an actor had to sign away the next five years of his or her career in order to *audition* for a part. The actors who didn't get chosen to be on the soap were freed from the contract, of course. But the ones who were cast were contractually obligated to a good, long run on the soap . . . as long as the soap wanted them. For some actors, like Dallas, this was a pretty scary step. But others, like Amelia, were more than willing to make the leap. None of them—not even Amelia—thought they'd stay on a soap opera forever. But most saw the soap as a good first step to something bigger.

"Is your mom back yet?" Amelia asked me now.

"No. Not 'til tomorrow."

"So invite him over. Tonight."

"Wait—one minute you're telling me not to see him, and now you're telling me to have a sleepover?"

"I said no such thing!" Amelia pretended to be shocked. "All I'm saying is: Give yourself the home-court advantage. For whatever happens."

This, I felt, made sense. Anywhere else we went—the movies, the mall, downtown—could be somewhere Keith had been with Erika. My house was the only place I could be sure was entirely mine. Her ghost wouldn't be able to get its bearings.

Before I could chicken out, I texted him to ask if he was free tonight.

Fifteen seconds later, I had his reply:

4 U? OF COURSE.

I hated myself for how happy that made me.

The happiness, however, was temporary. As I waited for him to come over, it was bumped down the charts by anxiety. I knew I had to talk to Keith—really talk to him—but I had no idea which words to use.

It didn't help that he looked about as cutesexy as can be when I opened the door—with the cutesexiest part being how happy he was to see me.

"Hey, Ophelia," he said.

"What's up, Hamlet?" I replied.

I was trying to keep it casual, but the result of that was we casually fell back into our usual patterns. Meaning: It wasn't two seconds after the door closed that we were mashing up against each other, kissing our hellos.

"Where've you been, Athena?"

"Just busy, Adonis."

Moving over to the couch.

"I've missed you, Rhett," he said.

"Yeah, Scarlett."

How long had I waited for some guy to call me his Rhett Butler?

There we were, maneuvering into position for The Long

Cuddle. Part of me pleading to myself, *Don't think about the mall.* The other part reminding me, *The mall, the mall.*

He wasn't mentioning her. He wasn't with her. He was with me. I should have been happy. I should have been able to ignore it.

But instead I sat up and ruined The Long Cuddle.

"Holmes . . . ," I began.

Keith looked at me quizzically.

"What is it, Watson?" he asked.

All of a sudden, it was like I was filled again by the sad emptiness. All my joy was hollowed out.

And I couldn't. Say. A thing.

Keith looked at me more seriously now.

"What?" he asked again. "Tell me."

I wanted to make a joke of it, since it was making such a joke out of me.

"Guess who I saw the other day," I said.

"Elvis?"

"No, Keith. I saw you and Erika. Together at the Beverly Center."

"Oh."

He didn't say, *Why didn't you come over and say hi?* or *I was only there because her therapist said I had to be* or *Are you sure it was me?* He knew better than to try any of those. Which made it harder to be mad at him and therefore easier to be sad.

"I know it's not fair," I went on. "It's not like you've ever lied to me. You haven't. But to actually see the two of you together . . ."

"It hurt?"

"Yeah, it hurt. A lot."

168

Keith leaned into me and stroked my hair.

"I'm so sorry," he said. "I would've rather been there with you, Romeo."

It would have been so easy to leave it there. It would have been so easy to let him stroke my hair and kiss me again and make out a little and forget about Erika and keep doing what we'd been doing, in the hope that one day she'd be out of the picture and I would be in it—in the foreground, in the center. But it was like this was the one thing too many, the one brick that made the relationship too heavy to carry. I couldn't do it.

"No," I said, turning away, staring at the dead television on our wall. "I can't do this, Keith. I'm sorry. We can't keep doing this."

"Mallory," he said, putting his arms around me and nuzzling into my neck. "Mallory. . . ."

That's when I surprised both of us—by pushing him away, by standing up, by ending everything.

"You don't get it, do you?" I asked, somewhere between a plea and a yell. "I am always, *always* thinking of you being with her. That whenever you leave me, you just go back to her. And it kills me, Keith. It *kills* me. I know you're trying to do the right thing. I know that you're at heart a great guy. I would love to be with you. But I can't do it like this. It's not fair to me, and it's not fair to her. Although, honestly, I don't really care about her. Mostly, I care that it's not fair to me."

Keith finally understood what was happening here, and it hit him hard. Suddenly he woke up from his dreaminess and became a complete mess.

"Can't we figure it out?" he asked. "I mean, are we just over?"

No-yes, I thought. *Yes-no.*

"I'll break up with Erika," he said. "She's really fragile right now, but—"

"No," I said. "You've said that before. And the perverse thing is that I can understand that she needs you. But that means I can't need you, too."

"But I need *you,*" Keith insisted. "I do."

How rare is it to hear these words? How often would I have someone ask me so desperately to stay? I couldn't ignore the fact that even while I was letting go, it meant something to me that he was fighting to hold on.

"You need to go now," I said. "We could talk about this for days, but we'll only be saying the same things over and over. And I don't think either of us could stand that."

But he just sat there on the couch, looking helpless.

"Come on . . . ," he said.

I shook my head. I knew he could wear me down. I knew he could make me doubt it. So if he wasn't going to leave, I had to.

"I'm going to go upstairs," I told him. "Let yourself out, okay?"

I disappeared into my own house. I hid in my own bedroom. I stayed perfectly quiet, waiting until I heard the sound of the door closing behind him.

Then I let myself be a total mess, regretting everything.

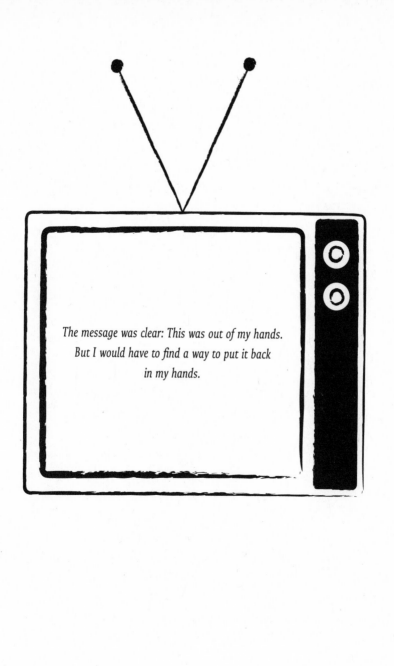

The message was clear: This was out of my hands. But I would have to find a way to put it back in my hands.

s e v e n t e e n

Amelia assured me I had done the right thing by breaking up with Keith. But it was a measure of how badly I was taking it that she still had to assure me a week later, as Jake drove both of us to the studio. It was the day of Amelia's big last-round audition, and while I liked to think that I was just distracting her from her nerves by talking all about me, the truth was that I needed the talking more. Poor Amelia—now that I didn't have Keith, she was the only person besides Gina that I could confide in.

All the talking stopped when we got to the studio. Amelia wanted to get into actress mode before her audition scenes. And I—well, I bumped into Dallas.

Richard and Annie had flown him in to read with all the possible Sarahs and Jacquelines. I knew this. But still it was a shock to see him. So much had happened to me since we'd been at the Getty. But he didn't know any of it. Because, at heart, we were still strangers.

"Hey, Chekhov!" he called out when he saw me.

Hey, Shakespeare! I almost called back. But then I realized: He wasn't Keith. We weren't playing the nickname game.

So instead I just said, "Hey," and we walked over to each other. An awkward moment followed—were we supposed to hug? Shake hands? Curtsy? In the end, we just smiled and asked each other how things were going. A few weeks ago, even this basic exchange would have made my heart flutter. But now my heart was saying, *I'm just too exhausted right now to flutter. I would if I could. Sorry.*

"You ready for all of the Sarahs and Jacquelines?" I asked.

"One of them's your best friend, right?"

I hadn't told him this. Who'd told him this?

I figured it would be silly to deny it.

"Yeah—Amelia. Be nice to her."

"Amelia. Cool."

Annie's assistant Phil came over and explained to us what would happen: Each actress would do two scenes with Dallas, one as Sarah and one as Jacqueline. There would be three cameras taping, and Tillman Lane, one of the *Good As Gold* directors, would be directing. Once the taping was done, the footage would be edited into a scene (just like it would have been for a real show), and then all of the scenes would be put on a tape for everyone to take a look at before the big-decision conversation occurred.

We were actually taping on one of the *Good As Gold* sets that wasn't being used that week—Brick and Loni Madison's bedroom. Because my mother's character, Geneva, hadn't been involved with Brick or friends with Loni for quite a while, I didn't really have many associations with the room itself. Still, it was strange to be bringing my characters into my mother's world. I expected us to be kicked out at any moment.

"I grew up here," I told Dallas.

"In this very room?" he joked.

"Yeah. I didn't know rooms were supposed to have four walls until I was old enough to leave."

Dallas chuckled, and I was starting to feel better about life in general when suddenly there was a voice behind him.

"Dallas?" it asked—and Dallas immediately responded. He half turned, then opened his arm out so a stellarly beautiful girl could be held by it.

"Mallory, have you met Francesca?"

"No," I said, wedging up a smile on my face. "It's so great to meet you."

"You too," Francesca said, offering a hand. It was so dainty and porcelain that I almost feared to shake it.

"Francesca's auditioning today," Dallas explained. "But I guess you already know that."

Yes, I knew all about Francesca Moore. And it was even worse face to face.

"They're calling for you both on the set," Francesca said. "It's almost time to start shooting. Tillman looks like he's ready to start taping."

"You know Tillman?" I asked.

"No," Francesca replied. "We just met. But he's really great."

So she was already buddies with the director.

This was bad news.

And the way that Dallas kept his arm around her was bad news, too.

Richard, Annie, and I were watching the auditions from the control room, with Phil as our messenger and Tracy keeping the other actresses company. (They would *not* be seeing one another audition.) Since the boom mics were open, we could hear everything that was said on the set.

Francesca was the first up. She and Dallas talked quietly as Tillman set up all the shots. I tried not to look.

"Pay attention," Richard told me, pointing at Francesca and Dallas. "This part is as important as the rest. You can tell whether they'll have chemistry or not."

Well, there was no doubt that Francesca and Dallas had chemistry—the kind of chemistry that was producing a poison in my gut. It was clear to me that they'd practiced the scenes together when they were back in New York, just like Amelia and I had been practicing here in LA. The difference was that while I was worse than amateur when it came to acting, Francesca and Dallas had perfected the rhythm of their scenes.

But perhaps they had perfected it too perfectly. . . .

Francesca and Dallas were great together, but I thought it was clear: Francesca was no Sarah. She was too glamorous, too beautiful. There was nothing vulnerable about her. You'd never imagine Dallas—I mean, Ryan—leaving her for anyone else.

She was better at being Jacqueline, who was a little bit colder and much more scheming than Sarah.

"She'd be a good Jacqueline," I said when the audition was through. "Not a Sarah, though."

"Shush," Richard told me. "No comments until we see the edited tape. Right now, you're watching a stage production,

176

seeing it live. But we're not casting them for a play—we're casting them for a TV show. So we need to see how it plays on TV before we come to any conclusions."

He said this like it was the most obvious thing in the world. *I'm new at this,* I wanted to say. But at the same time I knew it wasn't in my best interest to point it out.

I couldn't, however, help but laugh a few times when it was Genna's turn to audition. For one, Dallas didn't know *what* to do with her and the WAY she spoke her LINES. Also, her reading comprehension sometimes seemed to dip to *The Cat in the Hat* levels. She was doing a more than adequate job of acting with her cleavage, but (at least for me) her cleavage didn't have very much interesting to say.

Next, it was Alexis's turn. Once again her mother was demanding to be on the set during the audition, and once again Annie had her barred. Part of me wanted to slip out and meet this famous screaming mother, but since my attention was needed for the taping, I instead just pictured my own mother out there, making just as much fuss.

Dallas and Alexis chatted a little bit before the taping, and I could tell right away that there wouldn't be too much off-set chemistry here—Alexis was just too shy. As Dallas put on his charms, Alexis kept her eyes on her shoes, nodding every now and then, smiling carefully when she did manage to look him in the eyes. Finally, the stage manager called her on set and showed her how the scene was going to play out. She nodded once, said she didn't have any questions, and the taping began.

The transformation wasn't instantaneous. She didn't suddenly become a brazen knockout or a great comedian. But it became remarkably clear that Alexis not only understood Sarah but knew exactly how she'd sound and move. The chemistry that wasn't there before suddenly materialized—not in a sexy way but instead in a real way. Watching Alexis and Dallas act it, I could believe that Sarah and Ryan had been in love with each other for a while . . . and were now falling apart.

SARAH

When something happens to me,
you're the one I want to
tell. How do I erase that?
It's an impulse, Ryan. How do
you erase an impulse? How do
you make something that seems
so natural go away?

RYAN

I don't know, Sarah. I don't
know. All I can do is beg you
to forget me.

SARAH

But now I'm going to remember
you telling me to forget. You
keep trying to erase, but you
only write more.

RYAN

How many times do I have to
tell you it's over?

SARAH
Before I believe it?

RYAN
Yes. Before you believe it.

SARAH
I'd have to want to believe
it. In which case, we're both
in trouble.

I had written these lines. I had revised them at least a dozen times. I had read them over and over again with Amelia as we'd rehearsed. And still—it was like I was hearing them for the first time. *Seeing* them for the first time. And I got it, where these words were coming from. You think you're writing fiction, but it ends up that it's just pieces of your life that are coming out.

Alexis was also good as Jacqueline, but she didn't seem to understand the part and the motivations as well as she understood Sarah's.

When she was walking back to her mother in the waiting room, Richard said, "Damn, she's good!"

"I thought we weren't supposed to be drawing conclusions," I protested.

"Well, I know how things transfer to screen. And that, my friend, is going to transfer well."

I was glad that it was Stacy, and not Amelia, who was next. As if she sensed that someone better than her had been on the set just a few minutes before, Stacy never really calmed down. She rushed her lines, accidentally hit Dallas in the face when she was supposed to be patting him on the shoulder, and blanked during one of Jacqueline's pivotal moments. She was near tears by the time it was over.

"Next!" the stage manager called.

Amelia came in and made a beeline to Dallas, shaking his hand and flirting mercilessly. Maybe the others couldn't tell she was flirting, but I knew her style, and I knew what she was doing. It wasn't a serious flirt, but it was enough to make me feel a little weird. I had kind of wanted to be there when Amelia met Dallas; it seemed strange that they were talking together without me. In any other circumstance, I would have gone over and talked with them both. But I knew Richard was watching, and I didn't want him to continue to connect Amelia with me.

Tillman walked her through the shots just like he'd walked everyone else; since she'd never had to do a scene for the cameras before, it took Amelia a little longer to get the hang of it. The first time she and Dallas ran through it, she kept turning in the wrong direction or overacting in a way that would work for long shots but would be deadly for close-ups.

But that, really, wasn't the hardest part for me to watch. I'd been worried that when the time came, Amelia would seem too much like Amelia for me to really judge her as Sarah. But now that she was doing it, Amelia wasn't playing herself.

No, instead she was playing me.

It took me a minute or two to catch on. There had been a few times when we'd been rehearsing that Amelia had asked me to read Sarah's lines while she read Ryan's—just so she could understand his part, too, she said. But now I realized what else she'd been doing—she'd been catching my intonations as Sarah and was now trying to replicate them. Because, quite simply, she thought I was the character. And if she could imitate me well, she'd get the part.

It was too late to tell her that when I read Sarah's lines to myself, it wasn't my own voice I heard. It was someone else's.

Amelia's Sarah was a wreck—the kind of person who sees herself as devoted but is seen by everyone else as needy.

Is that how you really see me? I wondered.

Then I forced myself to remember it was just a character. Amelia was playing a character. In my voice.

There was no way I could objectively judge Amelia's performance. Instead I looked at Dallas when it was over. He didn't seem nearly as aghast as he was after Genna or as sympathetic as he was after Stacy blew it. But he didn't seem as enamored as he was with Francesca or as inspired as he was with Alexis.

Next, Amelia had to read as Jacqueline, and even I had to admit that she bombed. Instead of trying to act like me, she seemed to me trying to act like my mom, and it just didn't work. A sixteen-year-old playing a forty-five-year-old playing a sixteen-year-old might have worked for a comedy (especially one watched by gayboys), but it wasn't working for this audition. The good part was that clearly Amelia didn't want the part—she wanted Sarah's.

When it was all over, everyone thanked Amelia and Amelia thanked everyone. Then she was off, heading back home alone since I had to stay to talk to Richard and Annie. Dallas, too, hovered around until it was clear that nobody was going to ask his opinion. Then he and Francesca said good-bye to me and went off together.

"You think they're a couple?" Richard asked me.

I tried not to growl in reply.

"Well," Annie said, "that went well. I think we definitely have our girls here."

I didn't ask her which ones. But I had a sinking suspicion that she wasn't talking about Amelia.

Later on when Richard and I were alone for a second, I reminded him of my one demand.

"Amelia has to be Sarah," I told him. "I don't care who's Jacqueline. But Amelia's the one I'm writing Sarah for."

"Are you so sure?" he said. "Why don't you try writing now and see who comes to mind the most?" He studied my reaction. "Okay, so you're sticking to your guns. I admire that—to a point. We'll see the tapes, and then we'll all decide."

The message was clear: This was out of my hands.

But I would have to find a way to put it back in my hands. For Amelia's sake.

"Evil!" I cried out. "You're evil!"
His grin grew wider.
"We all have our calling," he said.

e i g h t e e n

That night I went over to Amelia's house. Even Jake seemed to be in a happy mood.

"She thinks it went well," he said to me while she went to get some sparkling grape juice to toast with. "Did it?"

"She was great," I assured him. "Really great."

When Amelia got back, she asked me when the actual decision would be made.

"Soon," I said. "Probably real soon. I don't think they're going to ask any other actresses to audition."

"Wish me luck!" Amelia said.

And I wondered: Why had that simple request become so complicated?

When I got home, I tried to work on a new script. I tried to picture Amelia as I was writing Sarah.

But Richard was right: Other faces were creeping in.

I shoved them out.

Amelia was my best friend. She would be my Sarah.

Mom was back in the house, but I couldn't talk to her. She was in storm mode, and I kept out of the way and waited for it to blow past. I had no doubt that her advice would be to cut Amelia loose. Which only made me want to hold on more.

Work is work, she'd say. *Don't make it personal.*

But life was personal. And work had to do with life. There was no separating them, not at this point.

I wanted to talk to someone. But I couldn't call Keith. And Dallas and I hadn't made it to that point. Especially not with Francesca around.

I started to panic. My body started to freak out.

Richard called. I shouldn't have answered. But I did.

"What is it?" I asked, my voice cracking.

"Are you on drugs?" he asked back.

"Why? Does it sound like I'm on drugs?"

"Either that or you've been sucking at the teat of a Red Bull."

"Bulls don't have teats, Richard. And I'm just panicking. No biggie."

"Oh lord—I hadn't realized we'd placed the panic button so close to your cradle."

"Is that a young joke, Richard?"

"It could be interpreted as such. Especially by someone who's panicking."

"If you want me to start making the old jokes, just give me the word. I can start calling you Middle-Aged Richard at any moment."

"Touché. How about you get some sleep? I believe it's

been known to have a positive effect when dealing with stress."

"How would you know? You don't sleep."

"I sleep all the time. Just never when you're around."

"Richard, why did you call?"

"The tapes will be ready tomorrow."

With that sentence, he guaranteed my night would be sleepless.

Keith tried to call. I set his number to its own ring, so I wouldn't answer.

The next day at school, Scooter told me all the soap-opera sites were abuzz about big changes at the networks. There was some gossip that *Good As Gold* might be failing. This, I figured, explained my mother's bad mood.

I asked Scooter if there was any gossip about *Likely Story*.

"There was one blogger who had this headline: '*Likely Story: Likely Happening?*'"

I panicked some more.

Richard called me again that afternoon.

"The tapes are in. I'm having a copy brought over to you. Watch it a few times, make your opinion, then you'll come in tomorrow and we'll discuss."

An hour later, Greg was at my door with the disc.

"Trip let you out of his sight?" I asked him.

He smiled and nervously loosened his already loose tie.

"They don't trust the messenger services anymore," he said. "It all ends up on YouTube."

He handed over the DVD, and I realized I didn't want him to leave. I didn't want to do this alone. "Do you want to come in and watch with me?" I asked him.

He shook his head. "I'm under strict orders: Drop this off and tell you to watch it alone."

"What if I never told?" I said.

He exaggeratedly looked around, as if there were spies in all of the hedges. "Your mom at home?"

I shook my head.

"Good," he said. "Because she scares the crap out of me."

"I'm going to tell her you said that," I joked.

He turned paler than paper.

"Kidding," I said.

"Yeah, warn me about that ahead of time from now on, okay?"

I led him straight to the den. He was clearly in awe of his surroundings. I wanted to tell him we'd never even made the Star Maps that tourists buy for their Hollywood vacations.

"You've got lovely eaves," he said.

"Well, that's the first time a boy's ever said that to me," I said back.

He blushed. I put the DVD into the player and . . . stressed. I positioned myself on the couch. Held out the remote. Pressed PLAY.

"Here we go," I told Greg.

"Wheeee!" he cried.

"No discussion until we've seen it all," I warned him.

"I wouldn't dream of it."

"And no hanky-panky."

"I think you're safe."

After an endless disclaimer about how people not supposed to be watching it shouldn't be watching it, the reel began. The editor had done a fantastic job—each audition now looked like it was part of an actual episode, with long shots and close-ups and different angles within each scene. There were the same edits for each audition, so the only thing different would be the actresses' performances. I almost felt like I was in my mother's position now—sitting on the couch, watching my own work (even if I myself wasn't on the screen). I was amazed at how easily Dallas transferred his charisma from life to screen; the fact that he was on an HD screen didn't stop my blood from moving a little bit quicker at the sight of him.

Down, girl, I thought. *You're here to focus on the Sarahs and the Jacquelines, not the Ryan.*

Francesca, I was happy to see, didn't come across well as Sarah. Although she was beautiful, it was an icy beauty, and I didn't find myself caring about her problems while she let them all out.

The qualities that doomed her as Sarah worked in her favor for Jacqueline. She came across as heartless, manipulative—someone you want to root against.

Alexis was Francesca's opposite—warm where Francesca was cold, sympathetic where Francesca was psychopathic. This wasn't what I was hoping for. I didn't want her to be that good. The pit in my stomach started moving to my brain.

Genna and Stacy were both disasters—for some reason, I'd been afraid that Genna's stupendous feats of mangled

189

articulation would somehow translate into something TV-worthy, but instead she seemed like a bad translation of a human being.

Then it was time to watch Amelia. I swore to myself that I'd be objective. I'd watch her audition like I didn't know her. I'd judge her purely on her merits.

That lasted for about two seconds.

I watched Amelia as Sarah once. Then a second time. Then a third time. I checked out her chemistry with Dallas. I pondered her acting ability. I imagined her in the other scenes as Sarah.

All my observations pointed to the same conclusion:

Amelia was good.

Not great. Not bad.

Good.

So then the question became: Was good really good enough?

It was, I figured, a matter of priorities. Which was more important to me—my best friend or having the best possible person play Sarah? Because I liked to think of myself as the kind of best friend who would put the friendship first, I knew what I had to do.

Good would have to be good enough.

"So what do you think?" I asked Greg when it was all over.

He mimed locking his lips and throwing away the key.

"What?" I said. "You're not allowed to say?"

"Rrrp mmmd ulw hmm," he replied.

"Unlock your lips."

He did.

"Trip would kill me. I'm not even supposed to be here, remember?"

I wanted to ask him about Amelia . . . but suddenly I was afraid. Afraid that he'd tell me she was bad. And also a little afraid that he'd spread word back that I had doubts.

"Fair enough," I told him. "You were never here."

"But I had a good time while I wasn't here," he said, standing up. "I'll tell them I got caught in traffic."

"Thank God for traffic," I said.

"I'm sure you'll make the right choices," he told me before he left.

And I thought, *But how well do you know me, really?*

When Amelia called me that night, she asked if I'd seen the tapes.

I told her she was great.

I told her she was going to be a star.

I told her we were in this together.

She said she'd never, ever been happier. And that made it all worth it for me.

I thought about it for about two seconds. Then I went in my mother's room, found the page in her address book reserved for her exes—I think she liked having them on a list with each other—and gave Trip a call.

Annie walked into Richard's office,
followed by Tracy and Phil.
"Oh my," she said, looking at me and Richard.
"Have we already jumped to the conflict stage?"

n i n e t e e n

"What were you thinking?!?" Richard shouted. "How could you be so blind to how this would play out? This could ruin us all!"

Richard, it appeared, was not taking my decision well.

"Don't you think you're being a little melodramatic?"

"You should *not* have told Trip Carver your preferences before you talked to me."

"I didn't tell him my *preferences*, Richard. I told him that I *insisted* on Amelia being cast as Sarah. You make it sound like I gave him a choice."

It didn't quite play out that way—it was really a friendly conversation between Trip and his former stepdaughter. And I'd done it before I talked to Richard because I knew this was how Richard was going to react.

"You can't seriously tell me you think she is the best actress for the role," Richard said. "The last time I checked, you still had eyes and ears that were in working condition."

His face was so red that I felt if I reached over and loosened the top button of his shirt, steam would come out.

At this point, Annie walked into Richard's office, followed by Tracy and Phil.

"Oh my," she said, looking at me and Richard. "Have we already jumped to the conflict stage?"

"Mallory has already talked to Mr. Carver and has *insisted* that her *friend* Amelia be given the part of Sarah," Richard said.

"Is that so?" Annie said, sitting down and gesturing for the rest of us to do the same. "Why don't we discuss this first, before we reach any conclusions."

Phil put the audition tape into the player in Richard's office, and we watched it yet again.

When it was through, Annie said, "I've been doing this for thirty years now. I like to think I know what I'm doing. But even still, I talked at length with Tracy and Phil about it, soliciting their opinions. And we all agree: Alexis is the best Sarah and Francesca is the best Jacqueline."

"But what about Amelia?" I asked.

Annie looked at me patiently. "Amelia is a good actress, Mallory. And it's possible we can find a smaller part for her. But she doesn't have, at this point, either the experience or the talent to be the lead in a soap opera. It would not just be unfair to the show, but it would be unfair to her to put her in such a position. I've seen girls break under much less strain than that."

"She can take it," I said.

"You see how stubborn she's being?" Richard complained.

"Quiet, Richard," Annie reprimanded. Then she turned to me. "Mallory? Look me in the eye, Mallory."

There wasn't any way to avoid it. I looked her straight in the eye.

"Do you think Amelia is the best person for the role?" she asked me.

"I think she's good enough," I replied.

Annie nodded, then continued. "So you're willing to risk not only your own show but the employment of hundreds of other people on 'good enough.'"

I didn't know what to say to that.

"Think about it," Annie told me. "We're meeting with the network tomorrow to discuss this and other plans for *Likely Story*. Hopefully we'll get the green light then."

"Haven't we already gotten the green light?" I asked.

Richard interrupted. "It's not like there's only one green light," he said. "It's more like a long road of traffic lights, and you hit 'em one by one."

"I'm trusting that you'll realize that it's always best to have the best person," Annie went on. "I plan on making my recommendations to the network, and I believe Richard will be making the same choices. You have to understand, Mallory: We know what we're doing. We are professionals. This is not meant to be condescending to you—I have no doubt that you are our equal in many areas, especially with your upbringing. But I think your motives are clouded right now, and while I was willing to humor your wishes until now, the time has come to make the choice that even you must realize is the right one."

I stayed silent as Annie, Richard, Tracy, and Phil listed the reasons Alexis and Francesca were the right choices. I could tell that they were really excited with the job they had done, and that they thought Alexis, Francesca, and Dallas would be the perfect leads.

Right before Annie left, she asked me again to think things over. Then she, Phil, and Tracy left me alone with Richard.

"Sometimes you have to betray the people who are close to you," Richard told me. Then he added, as an afterthought, "For their own good."

I didn't know what to do.

I was finding it hard to breathe. When I left Richard's office, I went to the little lounge room to take some deep breaths and calm down. Then I headed to the *Good As Gold* set.

I needed to talk to Gina.

Gina, however, wasn't in the mood to talk. She was, in fact, quite upset—which was not something I'd seen very often. Usually it took somebody's death to get her really upset.

"Oh, honey," she said sadly. "Everything's wrong."

I asked her what she meant, and she told me that all of the *Good As Gold* rumors were true—everyone at the network was telling her that the ax was soon going to fall.

"What am I going to do?" she asked.

I tried to imagine Gina outside of this dressing room, working somewhere else. It was really hard to do. She had made a home here. Everyone had made a home here. It made me realize how important work can be. A job, if it's the right job, can also be a home.

"We'll do something," I assured her. "Whatever we need

to do. I promise you'll be okay. I would never let anything bad happen to you."

It was so strange for me to be saying these things to her, after she'd spent what seemed like my whole life saying them to me.

"Where's my mother?" I asked her now. "Does she know?"

"She's home. And I think she does know. She hasn't been herself for weeks—you must have noticed."

I felt embarrassed to admit to Gina how little I saw my mother. And how little I knew about her. So I pretended that I *had* noticed.

"Don't you worry," Gina said, moving in for a hug. "Your mother always has a few tricks up her sleeve. I'm sure she'll be okay. I just hope she takes me with her!"

"She will," I said. "She's nothing without you."

Gina chuckled at that. I was glad I'd made her smile.

But I couldn't smile. There was too much going on. And suddenly I found myself asking Gina what I really needed to know.

"Gina," I said, "should the show always come first? I mean, if you had to choose between a friend and the show, what would you do?"

"You should try to make sure you're never in the position where you have to choose," she said. Then, looking at my face, she said, "That's not enough, is it?"

So I told her a short version of everything.

"Oh, sweetie," she said. "I can't tell you what to do there . . . but I'll bet you already know."

Yes, I wanted to say. *But the already knowing is killing me.*

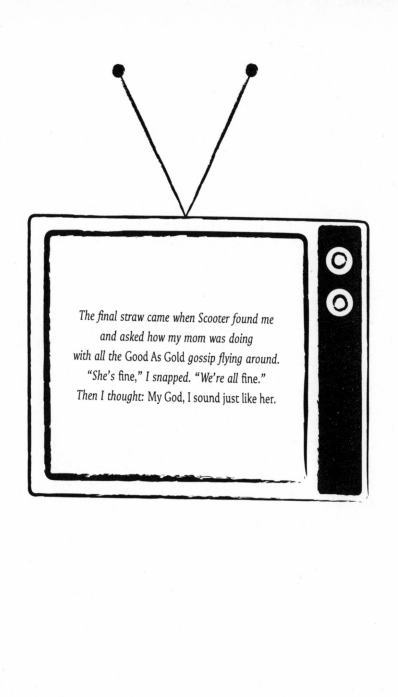

The final straw came when Scooter found me
and asked how my mom was doing
with all the Good As Gold *gossip flying around.*
"She's fine," I snapped. "We're all fine."
Then I thought: My God, I sound just like her.

twenty

When I got home, my mother was in her normal spot on the couch, watching herself on TV.

"Where were you?" she asked, not able to look away from the screen.

"At the studio," I said. "I just saw Gina."

"That's nice."

This could only be a cutting comment—my mother didn't believe in *nice*.

I tried for a moment to put myself in her shoes. A middle-aged actress on a low-rated soap opera facing unemployment for the first time in her adult life. I'd be scared. Or at least worried. This explained the sleepless nights. This explained the edge in her voice, and even her movements.

"Mom," I said, "are you okay?"

"Of course I'm okay," she answered stiffly. "Why wouldn't I be okay?"

It was like I'd *offended* her.

"No reason," I quickly replied. "Just asking."

She glared at me for a second. The meaning was clear: *What do you know?*

"Is *Good As Gold* okay?" I ventured.

"Don't worry about that," my mother said, wiping the question away. "It'll all be fine."

I sat down next to her on the couch. Even at home, she had makeup on. But it wasn't as neat as it was for the outside world. I could see the bags under her eyes. The worry wrinkles. The line on her neck where the makeup stopped and the real skin began.

She paused the program on the screen.

"What?" she asked.

"It's okay if you're worried," I said.

This made her laugh.

"Oh, that's *rich*. Thank you for telling me it's *okay*."

"God!" I yelled, standing back up. "I don't get you *at all*. Why can't you just fall apart like a normal person? Why do you have to hold yourself together by attacking me?"

She laughed again. "For someone who doesn't get me at all, you certainly have some theories."

"Mom. Your show is about to be canceled. That's what everyone's saying. I hear you up at night. I see you're only acting like everything's okay. Why can't you just admit it—you're scared."

This time the laughter was vacuumed up. Instead I got the chilliest of icy glares.

"I am. NOT. Scared," she said. "You don't have—and have never had—any appreciation for what it takes to be in this game. Which is why they're going to eat you alive. You see, Mallory, there are two types of people in television: the eaters and the eaten. I have always been an eater. You might not like that. You might hate it. But you know what? It's paid for your life so far, and it's going to continue to pay for your life. If you had any idea the things I've done for you, you would never treat me this way."

"What have you done? Tell me! I want to know!"

Mom shook her head. "No. You see, part of being a mother is not exposing you to such ugliness."

But I want to know you, I wanted to scream. *Don't you get that?*

She leaned back into the couch and picked up the remote.

"Don't worry," she told me. "I have everything under control."

"You're going to save *Good As Gold*?" I asked, thinking of Gina and everyone else on the set.

"If I don't save *Good As Gold,* I'm definitely going to save myself," she replied. "You can write that in platinum!"

"I get it," I said. "You're a fighter. I know that."

"Don't belittle me, Mallory. It won't get you anywhere."

"I wasn't belittling you," I mumbled.

"What? Speak up if you're going to say something to me."

I enunciated my next words very clearly: "NEV-ER MIND."

Mom shrugged—*Have it your way*—and unpaused her program. Geneva was back on-screen, wondering aloud if her experiments in voodoo had accidentally caused her lover's impotence.

"We never get anywhere, do we?" I asked.

Did she not hear me . . . or did she not have an answer? I couldn't tell.

I started to walk up to my room.

"Casting is important!" she called after me.

I turned back around.

"What?"

"I just wanted to tell you: Casting is important. Remember that."

"How do you know we're casting?"

"Mallory, I know everything."

"So who should I cast?" I challenged.

She raised an eyebrow. "Don't you already know?"

"I'm not really sure," I admitted.

"Well, if you don't trust yourself, ask someone you trust."

I wondered if she'd seen the casting tape. But did I really trust her? My gut told me she'd only pick the ugliest, most boring girls to be on the rival soaps, to make sure the competition was low.

"Thanks for the advice," I said.

"Anytime," she replied. Then she turned back to the TV.

My time was up.

As much as I hated to admit it, when I got back to my room, I realized she was right about one thing:

I had to talk to someone I trusted.

I debated it for a few hours. Then I called information and found out there was only one Dallas Grant in all of New York City. And his number was listed.

I thought about hanging up about two million times during the five times the phone rang.

"Hello?" he answered, his voice narcoleptic.

"Oh god, I'm sorry," I said. "I forgot about the time difference."

"Who is this?"

He didn't recognize my voice.

"Mallory. Mallory Hayden."

"Oh, hey, Mallory!" I could hear him sitting up in bed. "What's up?"

"I'm really sorry. I can call back—"

"No—it's cool. I was just, um, resting."

You know it's bad when the other person can't even make up an excuse.

"I just have a question. About Sarah. I mean, about the actress who should play Sarah."

"Um . . . have you guys decided?"

"No. So I was asking . . ."

"Well, it's not up to me."

"I know. I'm not entirely sure it's up to me, either. But you were there. You acted with all of them. Didn't you, um, have a preference? Take Amelia, for example. . . ."

"What are you doing?" Dallas asked, confused.

What answer could I possibly give him?

The truth wasn't an option. . . .

Or was it?

"Okay," I said. "Here's the thing. Amelia's my best friend. I promised her Sarah's part. But I don't think anyone else . . . wants that. So I need to talk to someone who I can . . . trust. Like you."

"How do you know you can trust me? I mean, I could do the same thing for Francesca that you're doing for Amelia."

"But you're not going to, are you?"

"No. I'm not."

I almost wanted to ask if Francesca was in the room with

207

him. Like, sharing the bed. But I didn't think she was. That wasn't the picture I had. The picture I had was so clear: Dallas all sleepy-haired in an old T-shirt and pajama pants, listening to me as his eyes got used to the dark.

"So what should I do?" I asked.

"Alexis was the best," he said. "Don't you think?"

"Yeah," I admitted, feeling like the worst friend in the world for saying it out loud. "She was pretty fantastic."

"Then that's your answer."

"It isn't that simple," I protested.

"Actually, Mallory, sometimes it is. I mean, if your boyfriend had auditioned for Ryan, I hope I still would've gotten the role."

"I don't have a boyfriend," I said. *Why was he saying I had a boyfriend?*

"Hypothetically, then. Your hypothetical boyfriend."

This, from the best possible hypothetical boyfriend I could think of at the moment.

"I hate this," I said.

"Amelia will understand," Dallas told me.

"You think?"

"Maybe not right away. But eventually. Believe me, you don't want the pressure if you can't handle it."

"And you don't think Amelia could handle it?"

"Not now, at least. But that's just my opinion."

"I trust your opinion."

"Thanks. I mean, that actually means a lot."

Yes, I thought, *it does mean a lot. Even if you don't really realize what it means exactly.*

"I should let you go," I said.

"Well, call back anytime. Nobody ever calls the house phone anymore. It can be like the red phone in the White House. It'll ring and I'll know it's you."

"Is the phone red?"

"What?"

"Your phone. Is it red?"

"No," he said sleepily, "but I promise I'll paint it tomorrow."

"Good night, Dallas."

"Good night, Mallory. You're good to care."

In that short second before we hung up, my heart was full of such a *Wish you were here* that I almost said it. Then I was glad that I didn't. And sad.

Finally, as I headed to bed, I realized:

He would be here soon enough.

Assuming the show went on.

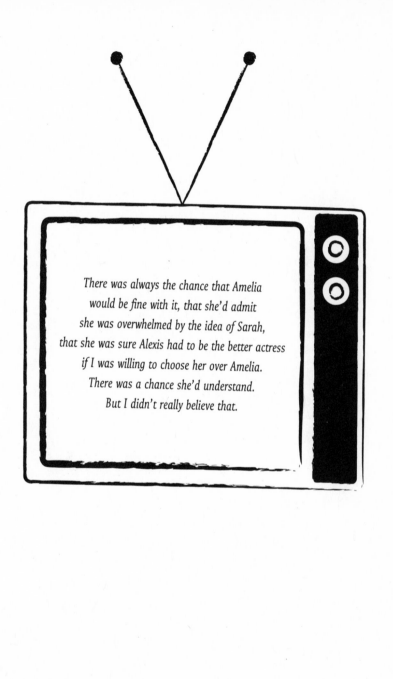

There was always the chance that Amelia
would be fine with it, that she'd admit
she was overwhelmed by the idea of Sarah,
that she was sure Alexis had to be the better actress
if I was willing to choose her over Amelia.
There was a chance she'd understand.
But I didn't really believe that.

twenty-one

I knew I had to tell Amelia myself.

But I also knew I couldn't do it in school.

By the time we got to her house after school, it was three.

My meeting with the network brass was at four.

Which gave me about a half hour, considering transportation time.

I spent the whole day in school feeling awful. It was clear that Amelia had already told a lot of her friends that she'd gotten the part. She was so happy about it.

In Holistic Spanish class, I felt like the walls were closing in on me.

In Unnatural Sciences, I seriously considered the fact that I'd probably have to switch schools to avoid seeing Amelia ever again, because the guilt would just kill me even if Amelia didn't do it with her own hands.

I felt like there was a tattoo across my forehead: I AM THE WORST FRIEND IN THE ENTIRE WORLD.

Amelia was close enough to see it. But she didn't. She couldn't read any of the signs.

She was too happy to notice. She just thought I was stressed about the meeting. About the changes the network was going to make.

She didn't realize she was one of those changes.

She didn't realize we were no longer going to be in this together.

I hadn't called Richard. I knew I should, just to get his guarantee that Amelia could get another, smaller role on the show. But I didn't want Richard (or anyone else besides Dallas) to know about my change of heart before Amelia did. I was already doing one unforgivable thing; I didn't want to make it worse by adding a few more.

There was always the chance that Amelia would be fine with it, that she'd admit she was overwhelmed by the idea of Sarah, that she was sure Alexis had to be the better actress if I was willing to choose her over Amelia. There was a chance she'd understand.

But I didn't really believe that.

To make matters worse, I saw Keith in the hallway near the end of the day. He saw me and started to come over, as if he had something to say to me. I couldn't take that—not now— so I ran away, just like I had at the mall. Only this time he was watching me run.

The final straw came when Scooter found me and asked me how my mom was doing with all the *Good As Gold* gossip flying around.

"She's *fine*," I snapped. "We're all *fine*."

Then I thought: *My God, I sound just like her.*

No matter how many times I apologized to Scooter, I couldn't erase that.

Finally, the school day was over. Amelia and I met up at her locker, and she spent the next fifteen minutes telling me about the fact that maybe, just maybe, this guy Doug on the swim team might want her to Marco his Polo. There was no natural way to switch the conversation to *Hey, I'm not giving you the part!*—so I just let it happen. Amelia's cluelessness made me even sadder.

We got to her house and received a grunted hello from Jake, who was playing some video game that seemed to require mass dismemberment. Charming.

"Let's go to the pool," Amelia suggested.

So I followed her back to the pool. It wasn't really swimming weather, but Amelia's family always kept the pool area prepped just in case it got too hot.

Amelia was about to start off on another topic when the decisive moment arrived in a text from Richard:

REMINDER: MTG IN 45 MIN. BE ON
TIME OR YOU WON'T BE A PART OF
THE DECISION MAKING.

"The decision making?" Amelia asked, reading over my shoulder. "So it'll be final today?"

"Yes," I said, putting my phone back in my bag and putting my bag down on one of the pool chairs.

"That's so exciting!" Amelia bubbled.

How can I do this to her? I thought.

215

Then I remembered:

You have to.

"Amelia . . ."

"I know I wasn't supposed to tell anyone, but I couldn't help it, and, I swear, the minute it's official I'm going to throw the biggest party—"

"Amelia."

"God, do you even know when we're going to start? I mean, they want it to be soon, right? Will I have any say in what Sarah wears? I mean, I know there's a costume person. But I have some ideas—"

"Amelia!"

"What?"

"There's something I need to tell you."

"I know, I know—I shouldn't have told everyone. But—"

"No. It's not that."

Finally, Amelia's mind seemed to switch gears from thinking about the future to thinking about the present.

"What is it, then?" She looked at me, and what I'm sure wasn't the most carefree of expressions crossed my face. "Are you okay?"

I should've rehearsed this part in my head. I should've searched for exactly the right words. I could have at least tried to find the easier way of doing this.

But no. Instead I just blurted, "You're not going to be Sarah."

She heard me. There's no way she couldn't have. But still she acted like I'd only mimed the words.

"What?" she asked.

"You didn't get the part. Alexis did."

"WHAT?!? They can't do that! Not to us. Not to *you*. This is *your* show."

"I know. But everyone agreed—"

"Threaten to quit! Threaten to take the show back!"

"I can't," I said. "I can't."

"Tell me it isn't true!" Amelia sobbed. "Please, tell me it isn't true."

I had no idea what to say. Instead I had the most awful thought: that even now, when Amelia was genuinely falling apart, it seemed like bad acting.

"You said everyone agreed," she sobbed. "You didn't agree, did you?"

I was going to lie. I was just trying to find the right way of phrasing the lie.

But I took too long.

"Oh no," Amelia said after I didn't respond immediately. "You couldn't. You didn't."

"I didn't!" I insisted. "I fought for you. But Richard and Annie and everyone else said Alexis was the best."

"And was she?"

"Yes. But I was going to make them cast you anyway."

Somehow when this was a thought, it seemed like the words of a good friend. It didn't sound that way out in the air, though.

"Oh, *thanks*," Amelia said, practically spitting the words out. "Clearly, you really fought it."

"Look," I said, "you got really far in the audition. I'm sure there will be another part—"

"I don't want another part! I want *Sarah!*"

Amelia was really crying now.

"This was supposed to be my big break, Mallory," she went on. "And you've ruined it. You've ruined it all!"

"It wasn't me!" I protested.

"Yes it was. I can see it on your face. The guilt, Mallory. You can't hide the guilt."

And she couldn't hide the fact that she was turning on me. The sadness was turning into anger . . . and I was the target.

"Why'd you get my hopes up, Mallory?" she asked. "Why'd you even bother? If you knew all along I wouldn't get the part, why have me humiliate myself by trying?"

"I didn't always know what would happen."

"Only when I auditioned, huh? Only when you saw how bad I was."

"You weren't bad! It's just that Alexis was . . ."

"Better. That's the word you're looking for, Mallory. *Better.*"

"It's not like that—"

"Then what's it like, Mallory? How 'bout this? You always get your way, and this time I was in the way of your way. It had to be about you. You can't act, but you still had to be the star. You act like you're boy poison, but you still have to be the one who gets Dallas."

Dallas?

"Dallas has nothing to do with this," I said.

"Sure," Amelia said. "I'm sure the fact that he and I had so much chemistry didn't bother you *at all.*"

"What are you talking about?"

Amelia actually laughed. "You're so transparent," she said, getting a little closer, in my face. "You saw you had competition and you eliminated it."

"That's ridiculous!" I said, taking a step back. "You're my best friend!"

"Mallory," she replied coldly, "I'm your *only* friend. And this is how you treat me!"

She stepped forward again, and I stepped back again. I wasn't thinking about it. I didn't notice that I was at the edge of the pool.

"I wanted you to get the part!" I cried.

"You've wrecked everything," Amelia shouted.

Then she stepped forward again.

And I stepped back.

Right into the pool.

For a second I didn't know what had happened. Then I was in the pool, feeling the shock of water, pushing myself back up, surfacing.

Amelia was just staring at me, sad and angry at the same time. And it was me saying the words that she should have been saying: "I'm sorry! I'm sorry!"

"I'm not sure you're sorry now," she replied. "But you will be. You're going to be *very* sorry."

"Don't!" I pleaded. I was standing up in the pool now, completely soaked. I should have gone to the side and pulled myself out, but I was genuinely afraid that Amelia would just kick me back in.

"I have to go now, Mallory. I have to go and call every single one of my friends and tell them that I didn't get the part that I told them I'd gotten. I have to tell my parents that my good friend Mallory sold me out for some other actress, and that the contract I signed and all the money it promised were complete lies. You always said it was our show, Mallory—*our* show. But it was always yours, wasn't it? Well, I hope you had fun using me. I have to tell you, you're really good at it. I never would have suspected that you'd do this to me at the end."

"I didn't mean to!" I told her.

"I should've known," Amelia said, going for one last stab. "You're your mother's daughter, through and through. You're *just like her.*"

And with that she stormed back inside. Leaving me shivering in the pool.

I wanted to chase after her. I wanted to explain to her what had happened. But I realized there was no way to do that without telling her over and over how she really wasn't good enough. Which wasn't what she wanted to hear. She had her own story to believe.

She wasn't a good enough actress.

And I wasn't a good enough friend.

That's what hurt the most: the truth of it. I *had* failed her. And now, it seemed, everything that I'd feared was going to come true.

My phone kept ringing. First it was Richard,
and I didn't pick up. Then it was Keith,
and I really didn't pick up. Once. Twice. Thrice.

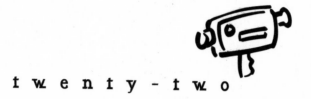

t w e n t y - t w o

I grabbed a towel out of the cabana and tried to dry myself off. I could hear my phone ringing in my bag.

"Hello," I said after fishing it out.

"Where are you?" Richard asked. "We're starting in twenty minutes. I wanted to talk to you before."

"I'm coming," I said.

"Don't be late," he warned. Then he hung up.

I walked back in the house. I went up to Amelia's room and knocked on the closed door.

"Go away!" she shouted.

"Come on, Amelia. Can't we just talk?"

"I said GO AWAY!"

Her voice was tear-clogged, and I would have done anything to unclog it. But clearly I wasn't going to make it past the door.

"Okay," I said gently. "But can we talk later?"

"NOT LIKELY!" she screamed.

I stayed there a minute longer, but all I could sense was her waiting for me to leave.

I knew I was totally late for what might be the biggest meeting of my life. It would take too long to call a cab. And there was no way to get Richard to send a studio car, since he thought I was already on my way.

I was at the front door when I realized what I had to do.

"Jake," I said, heading back to the living room and standing in front of the TV so he couldn't see his video game, "I need you to give me a ride."

He hit PAUSE.

"Let me get this straight," he said. "You ruined my sister's life, and you want a *ride*?!?"

"That about sums it up."

"Awesome!" he shouted. "Let's go."

It was not exactly a comfortable silence in the car.

"If you need to dry out those clothes," Jake said, "feel free to take 'em off and hold 'em out the window."

"No thanks," I replied.

My phone kept ringing. First it was Richard, and I didn't pick up. Then it was Keith, and I really didn't pick up. Once. Twice. Thrice.

"So," Jake said, "do you think I could get a part on your show? That would *really* kill Amelia."

I wrung the bottom of my shirt out on his car's upholstery.

When we got closer to the studio, Jake became more of a daredevil driver. I wasn't sure he was the particular devil that I wanted to dare, but I had to admit: The crazier he drove, the more likely it was that I wouldn't miss the meeting.

I tried to get Amelia out of my mind. I wanted to believe

that it would all blow over and that eventually she'd realize that I'd done the right thing.

But mostly I was feeling that would never happen. I'd seen a side of Amelia just now that I'd never seen before—fully vindictive, completely unforgiving. And now that I'd seen it, I couldn't take it out of my image of her. Once it was there, it would always be there.

"I totally just lost my best friend," I said out loud.

"I'll be your new best friend," Jake offered.

"Not what I was looking for," I told him.

"Offer's good for another two minutes, or until we hit that traffic light."

More calls from Richard. A text asking me where I was.

And then we were at the studio, making it through the gates. Despite the pulsing dread that seemed to fill every ounce of available space in my body, I also felt a good amount of relief.

"Here we go," Jake said, pulling over in a handicapped space by the building where I needed to be.

I unbuckled my seat belt.

"How can I thank you?" I asked.

"Like this," he said. Then he leaned over and kissed me. Hard.

"WHOA!" I shouted, pulling away. "Whoa whoa *whoa!*"

He grinned mischievously and said, "I can't wait to tell Amelia you did that."

"Evil!" I cried out. "You're *evil!*"

His grin grew wider. "We all have our calling," he said.

I jumped out of the car and slammed the door. I could tell he was laughing now, and I was going to leave him to it.

My phone rang with another text. Figuring it was from Richard and that I could text him back now, I took a look.

It wasn't from Richard. It was from Keith. And it had meant enough to him that he hadn't abbreviated a single word.

MALLORY—I HAVE FINALLY DONE IT. I HAVE BROKEN UP WITH ERIKA. SHE AND I ARE HISTORY. YOU AND I ARE HOPEFULLY THE FUTURE. IT IS OVER WITH HER. I AM PRAYING IT IS NOT OVER WITH YOU. I MISS YOU MORE THAN I WOULD MISS THE OCEAN OR THE SUN. WHICH IS A LOT. CAN WE TRY AGAIN? THERE IS ONLY YOU NOW. ONLY US.
LOVE, KEITH

"There you are!" someone yelled. I looked up from my phone, still a little in shock, and saw Greg. "I've been looking all over for you," he said. "They've just started."

I let him lead me forward, through the hallways. He didn't say anything about my wet clothes. He didn't even seem to notice.

I was letting myself go along with it all. But when we got close to the room and Greg said, "They're all in there," my legs wouldn't move.

"Mallory?" he asked.

"I can't," I said.

At first he looked panicked—not for me but for himself. His job was to get me to that meeting, and I was going to mess that all up. But then he took a real look at me. Saw me.

"Nothing makes sense," I said.

Gently, he put his hand on my shoulder.

"You have to pretend it makes sense," he told me. "They don't really know anything, either. It's all a matter of presentation."

I didn't tell him that the first time I'd ever seen him, he'd looked out of place in his suit. I didn't tell him that he was probably like me—in way over his head, dealing with adults who may or may not have his best interests at heart.

Instead I said to him, "When this is all over, can we be friends? Because I really need friends."

He smiled. "I'd like that."

"Okay," I said, taking a deep breath and releasing it. "I'd better get in there before we both get fired."

It's all a matter of presentation, I thought. And then I walked in.

"There she is!" Trip Carver called.

All eyes in the boardroom turned to me.

A matter of presentation.

"Wet is the new dry," I said, laughing about my clothes. "Sorry I'm late."

Richard had saved me a seat near him, but there was also an empty chair next to Trip.

I took that one.

"What's the story?" I asked Trip. Casual. Totally secure. Letting everyone else in the room remember: This guy used to be my stepdad.

"We're just talking about casting."

I looked at Richard, then at Annie.

"Alexis Randall for Sarah, Francesca Moore for Jacqueline,

and, of course, Dallas Grant for Ryan," I said. "Any questions?"

Richard looked relieved.

"No," Trip said. "Those were our choices as well. I'm glad we're all in agreement. That must mean something, since getting a room of executives to agree on anything is like trying to get an alligator to mate with a shark."

I had to bottle up all the nervous stress laughter at that one. *If I start letting anything out,* I thought, *I might never stop.*

Trip was now talking about how everyone was feeling really good about the script and the casting and the budget and the sets. Then the other network VPs chimed in about how great they thought it was, blah blah blah. I knew it was very important to be listening, but my mind was full of newsflashes.

NEWSFLASH: KEITH BROKE UP WITH ERIKA!

NEWSFLASH: AMELIA IS NO LONGER YOUR FRIEND!

NEWSFLASH: HER BROTHER KISSED YOU!

I looked over at Richard, and he seemed . . . uneasy.

BREAKING NEWSFLASH: SOMETHING ELSE IS GOING ON!

One of the VPs was talking about "a great opportunity"—and I'd missed what the opportunity was.

"As I've told you all along," Richard spoke up, "I agree that broadening our demographics is a brilliant idea."

"Well then—the show is a go," Trip Carver said. "On one condition."

One condition?

"What's that?" I asked, trying to pretend that everything made sense.

"As you have probably figured out, we are hoping to give

Likely Story the time slot that *Good As Gold* occupies, now that *Good As Gold* is going to be canceled. And Stu Eisenhorn had an idea—well, I think it's a brilliant idea. We've all discussed it, and we think it's just the thing to get *Likely Story* off the ground."

I turned to Richard. Clearly he knew what was going on. But he wouldn't meet my eye.

Trip continued. "We love Alexis, Francesca, and Dallas, and believe you've clearly found three stars who can take soaps far into the future. But that doesn't mean we have to ignore the past entirely. We can have it all—a show for adults *and* teens. A show for today *and* tomorrow. A show for mothers *and* daughters."

Trip stood up from the table and walked to the door.

"Ladies and gentlemen," he said, "I am proud to present you with the fourth star of *Likely Story*!"

And with that introduction, before I could even get a word out, my mother walked into the room.

"Every princess deserves to have a queen!" she purred.

Everyone burst into applause. Everyone but me. In that split second when all eyes were on her, I had to figure out a way to react.

There was no question about it: I'd been betrayed. I was shocked. Outraged. Indignant. Burning mad.

But I knew I couldn't let anyone see that.

This was a test. Perhaps *the* test.

I would not think about my mother. I would not think about how long she must've known that this was going to happen. I would not think about how she was behind the ambush.

Instead I thought about Gina.

Gina, who'd always been so nice to me. Gina, who hugged and supported me even when my mother didn't. Gina, whose show was about to be canceled and who would need a new job on a new show.

I could save her.

If *Good As Gold* was sinking, I could save as many people as possible. I could bring them all over to *Likely Story*.

The only hitch was that my mother would be in the lifeboat, too.

I looked over at Trip Carver. He was watching me. Challenging me. Seeing how I would react.

You can't throw me, I thought. *I'll show you how much I've learned.*

I put a big smile on my face—big enough to seem genuinely thrilled but not so big as to seem sarcastic. I walked over to my mother with open arms.

I am not an actress. But if there's one role I've been taught how to play, it's The Loving Daughter.

She was still basking in their applause. Then she saw me coming—and, I swear, for a moment there was fear in her eyes. I was suddenly unpredictable.

That's right, I thought. *Keep that fear there. You're going to need it.*

To keep the show, I'd play their game. And I'd win.

I hugged her then like I'd never hugged her before.

Then, loud enough so everyone could hear, I proclaimed: "Mom! Welcome to *my* show!"

Chris Van Etten graduated from NYU's Tisch School of the Arts with the intention of becoming an actor. Luckily, he came to his senses and became a writer for ABC's *One Life to Live* instead. As part of that writing team, he has been nominated for a Daytime Emmy and a Writers Guild of America Award. Despite his day job, he has just one personality.

Collectively, the authors would like to thank all of the remarkably kind people at Knopf, including Nancy Hinkel (our great show runner), Allison Wortche, and Melissa Nelson. Individually, David L. would like to thank his family and friends, especially Nick; David O. would like to thank Tom and Carol Ozanich, Diane Ozanich, Buck Drummond, Jennye Garibaldi, Liz Ureneck, Gray Coleman, and Chris Tuttle; and Chris would like to thank his mom and dad, Brian, and Nick, as well as his friends and colleagues at *One Life to Live,* without whom there would be no *Likely Story.*

To read more about David Van Etten, be sure to check out www.myspace.com/davidvanetten.

About the Authors

David Van Etten splits himself between three minds and three bodies. They belong to:

David Levithan has a newfound appreciation of soap operas because of Mallory and *Likely Story*. He's the author of a few books, including *Boy Meets Boy*, *The Realm of Possibility*, *Are We There Yet?*, *Marly's Ghost*, *Wide Awake*, *How They Met, and Other Stories*, and, with Rachel Cohn, *Nick & Norah's Infinite Playlist* and *Naomi and Ely's No Kiss List*. He lives in New Jersey. His identical twin was not separated from him at birth. Or so he thinks.

David Ozanich suffers from amnesia and may or may not have graduated from NYU's Tisch School of the Arts with degrees in film and dramatic writing. When not entangled in steamy love triangles, he makes films and writes plays. His play *The Lightning Field* premiered in New York and won the GLAAD Media Award, among others. His favorite band is Steely Dan.